THE HAYLEY MYSTERIES

THE MISSING JEWELS

THE HAYLEY MYSTERIES

THE MISSING JEWELS

HAYLEY LEBLANC

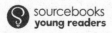

sourcebooks
young readers

Copyright © 2022 by Sourcebooks
Cover and internal design © 2022 by Sourcebooks
Cover design by Maryn Arreguín/Sourcebooks
Internal design by Michelle Mayhall/Sourcebooks
Cover and internal illustrations by Alessia Trunfio

Sourcebooks and the colophon are registered trademarks of Sourcebooks.

All rights reserved. No part of this book may be reproduced in any form or by any electronic or mechanical means including information storage and retrieval systems—except in the case of brief quotations embodied in critical articles or reviews—without permission in writing from its publisher, Sourcebooks.

The characters and events portrayed in this book are fictitious or are used fictitiously. Any similarity to real persons, living or dead, is purely coincidental and not intended by the author.

Published by Sourcebooks Young Readers, an imprint of Sourcebooks Kids
P.O. Box 4410, Naperville, Illinois 60567–4410
(630) 961-3900
sourcebooks.com

Cataloging-in-Publication Data is on file with the Library of Congress.

This product conforms to all applicable CPSC and CPSIA standards.

Source of Production: Versa Press, East Peoria, Illinois, United States
Date of Production: July 2022
Run Number: 5026294

Printed and bound in the United States of America.
VP 10 9 8 7 6 5 4 3 2 1

Dedicated to my sister Jules,

who always has my back, no matter what happens.

CHAPTER ONE

FLASHBULBS POP IN MY FACE. "SMILE, HAYLEY!" A PHOTOGRApher cries. "Hold that pose! Just like that! Amazing!"

I squeeze in with my two best friends, Aubrey and Cody. The three of us are wearing itchy tweed Sherlock Holmes detective hats and jackets, and I'm holding a huge magnifying glass that's the size of a cantaloupe. We're dressed this way because of the show we star in, *Sadie Solves It*. I play Sadie, the lead, who is so into solving mysteries that her catchphrase is "I eat clues for breakfast." That always makes me laugh. I can't help but imagine the clues in an alphabet soup and Sadie slurping them up with a spoon.

My best friends play Kiki and Markus, Sadie's mystery solving squad. *Fangirl Magazine* has come onto our set to photograph and interview us for a cover feature story. A cover! I've never been on the cover of a magazine, and neither have my friends, so we're all really excited.

A fourth actor on our show, Amelia Hart, nudges her way into the photo too. "Can't forget Pepper!"

"Oh, don't worry." I roll my eyes. "You make sure we *never* forget Pepper." While Cody is twelve and Aubrey and I are thirteen, Amelia is only ten. She plays Sadie's younger sister, Pepper, and she's eager to be included. She even whined her way into being in this photo shoot.

Actually, I bet Amelia's mom whined her daughter's way into the photo shoot. Mrs. Hart takes the term *Momager* to the next level.

"That should do it," says Bruce the photographer, a friendly guy with a bushy beard and wire-frame glasses. He checks the screen on the back of his digital camera. "These are great. I'll turn you over to Imogen now."

Imogen, *Fangirl*'s reporter, swoops over in her high heels and bright pink lipstick. We've met her a few times before. She visited our old set in Burbank, California, to talk to us during *Sadie Solves It*'s first season. Imogen is even nosier than Amelia, and that's saying a lot. She's always hunting for a good scoop, and she doesn't care how she gets it.

"Hey team!" Imogen cries, fiddling with her audio recorder. "It's been a while, huh? You need to fill me in on everything that's changed!"

My friends and I exchange glances. Since our last interview, our show has been renewed, and we've moved to a new set, Silver Screen Studios, which is in Hollywood.

But it's been rocky. Don't get me wrong, I adore Hollywood—zany Hollywood Boulevard with its Batman impersonators and junk shops and the area's rich history of moviemaking. The new set is also much closer to

the supersecret tree house in my family's backyard. But for a little while, none of us wanted to be at Silver Screen Studios at all.

"Give me the scoop," Imogen whispers, settling down on a bench. We're across the street from my trailer and the *Sadie* soundstage, where we shoot all of our interior scenes. (A soundstage is a big building that houses a whole bunch of inside sets. It's usually three stories tall, and *freezing*, because the filmmakers have to use so much lighting to make the scenes look real.) "I heard you've had some excitement on the new set? Something about...a *ghost*?"

Amelia breathes in to answer. I'm afraid she'll spill the beans about what happened, so I quickly say, "Oh, there were a few rumors going around. And as we all know, Hollywood has a history of being haunted! But we're all good."

Imogen widens her eyes. "I heard Amelia saw something pretty spooky. Can you tell us about it?"

"Amelia *thought* she saw something," Aubrey interrupts. Her tweed jacket has flecks of bright pink that looks great against her darker skin. Instead of changing into the loafers our wardrobe department suggested for this shoot, she insisted on wearing her slightly muddy soccer cleats. Somehow, Aubrey fits in a traveling soccer schedule along with filming the show *and* our many hours of private tutoring for school.

Imogen frowns. "Amelia can speak for herself."

Amelia's dark hair is in two braids. She's sitting with posture so perfect, she could probably balance a flowerpot on her head. She glances at us, and for once—to my relief—takes our lead on how to answer.

"Oh, *that*," she says with a serene smile. "It was nothing, really. Just a little mystery we solved."

"Wasn't it *you* who solved the mystery, Hayley?" Imogen asks. "Just like Sadie?"

"All I can say is that it was the four of us who solved the mystery," I say, looking at my friends—and Amelia too, because even though she's annoying, she had a role in tracking down some clues.

"Impressive, the way you all worked together," Imogen says. "I've always heard that people on sets don't get along. There's always a bad apple that spoils the bunch."

"Not here," Aubrey jumps in. "We're all besties. We have each other's backs."

"Totally," Cody adds, giving us a meaningful smile. During the ghost problem, it seemed our show might get shut down, and Cody's two moms were *this close* to pulling Cody out of LA and uniting the family back together in Texas. We were afraid we'd never see him again. But once the case was solved, Cody's moms and his little brother moved here instead. Their new condo rocks.

"Fine. *Don't* tell me." Imogen sighs. "I guess I can write about how you're all such best friends, then. But I have to say, that's a little *boring*."

"Boring is good," I tell her. "I'd rather nothing weird happen on set ever again."

"Same here!" Cody says.

"And we're starting a new episode today!" Aubrey says. "It's about a woman with a secret past who comes into town and needs Sadie to find her long-lost twin sister. She's being played by Brooklyn Bates."

"Uh huh," Imogen mumbles, as if Brooklyn Bates is some random actor and not the star of a million superhero movies. But I know why Imogen's disappointed. It doesn't matter that things are going really, really well on *Sadie Solves It*. It doesn't even matter that we're no longer in danger of being canceled or that Cody gets to stay in LA or that I still get to see one of my friends every day.

Nope. Imogen wants gossip. *Sorry, Imogen. Not today.*

Imogen checks her watch. "Out of time." She closes her notebook. "I'm sure I have enough to put together a cover article. Though if you want to add anything—anything about *ghosts*, maybe—you know where to find me." She winks.

After Imogen and Bruce head to their car, I look at my friends. "That went pretty well."

"Ugh, she's so pushy," Cody mutters, running a hand through his mop of white-blond curls. "It's a wonder she didn't go through our phones for random texts or something. Or through our backpacks for secret diary entries."

"Our backpacks?" Amelia's fingers fly nervously to a zippered pocket in the flowered backpack she carries everywhere.

Aubrey turns to me. "Can I stop in your trailer for a sec, Hayley? I baked Salmon some treats last night. Wanna see how he likes them!"

"Sure." Salmon is my black cat. The *Sadie* team is nice enough to let me bring him on set, mostly because everyone loves him and he totally fits with the spooky, mystery-solving vibe. Some people on set, like the makeup artist, Vee, even installed a cat door in her trailer so Salmon can come and go as he pleases.

We're just about to my trailer when we hear a loud

scream from inside the *Sadie* soundstage. Cody, Aubrey, and I exchange shocked looks. Lucinda, who works in the props department, sprints onto the pavement. Her frizzy hair is even taller and frizzier today, and she's trembling.

Paul, our show's creator, runs after her. A few writers, producers, and our director Monique follow. As soon as I see Paul's face, my stomach plummets. Something is *wrong*. I also notice Imogen freeze by her car, eyeing the scene with interest.

"What is it?" I ask, rushing over to Lucinda. "What's happened?"

"I can't find a major piece of jewelry for this episode," Lucinda cries. "It's been *stolen*!"

CHAPTER TWO

"STOLEN?" PAUL HURRIES TO LUCINDA'S SIDE. "ARE YOU
sure?"

"I had it sitting on my desk, and now it's gone."
Lucinda looks worried. "Those jewels were expensive!"

Paul looks like he's going to say something else, but
then he pauses, noticing Imogen the reporter creeping closer.

"Nothing to see here!" he shouts at her. "I'm sure it'll
turn up." Then he ushers Lucinda back toward the soundstage and out of earshot.

Aubrey's head swivels to watch Paul take Lucinda

into the big set of buildings where the props department office is. "What do you think happened?" she whispers.

"I don't know," I murmur. "Want to find out?"

Cody looks worried. "What about our lines? I don't have mine memorized yet."

"And that'll take you, what, five minutes?" Besides being a whiz with numbers and computer coding, Cody has a photographic memory. He learns his lines the first time he reads them.

"I'm in," Aubrey says.

"Yeah, okay," Cody agrees. "Let's go see what's up."

I turn to Amelia, figuring she'll want to tag along, but she's gone.

We head into the office building and up the stairs toward the props room. We're not spying, exactly, but Paul has ordered the three of us not to get involved in any more mysteries on the set. I know he's grateful that we solved the ghost problem, but I think he wants us to concentrate on our jobs first and foremost.

Still, a robbery? This is juicy.

The door to the props room is half open, and we can hear rustling, clanging, and banging inside. Lucinda is overturning boxes of props, looking for whatever has gone missing. Paul helps too. The props are well organized, but for whatever reason, Paul is looking in a bin marked "Giovanni's Pizza Shop." He pulls out checkerboard tablecloths, plastic soda cups, paper menus, and a chef's hat.

"So which piece was it?" Paul murmurs.

"The diamond tiara the princess wears in those early scenes, when she comes back into town," Lucinda says.

I exchange a look with my friends. The mysterious woman in this episode is a princess? I didn't read that in the script.

"Diamonds?" Paul asks. "How much is it worth?"

Lucinda shuts a drawer I usually love going through—it's filled with keys of all shapes and sizes. We need a *lot* of spooky keys in *Sadie Solves It*. "It's just paste, but still," she says.

Paste is a type of jewelry that's made out of a special glass that looks like real gemstones. It's been around for centuries, and some of it is really beautiful, and I have no doubt Lucinda found an amazing piece for the princess's tiara. Last season, Sadie wore a necklace that was also paste—she'd gotten it as a gift from a wealthy woman who lived in a haunted house after Sadie figured out that she wasn't being visited by a ghost but by a noisy family of raccoons. For a while, I wore the necklace on the show, but we figured out that the necklace jangled too much and messed with the sound in some of the scenes. Now, Sadie wears a special ring as her signature piece. I spin it around my finger now, admiring the authentic-looking sapphire set on the band. This piece is paste too.

Paul slams a drawer and groans. "This'll set us back. We shot some of Brooklyn's scenes last week because it was the only time she could fit it in her schedule. Now that the crown is gone, we'll have to reshoot. Or maybe try and edit around it?" He starts to vigorously rub his earlobes. Uh-oh. When Paul massages his ears, it means he's really worried.

Then, Cody lets out a sneeze. It sounds like an elephant even though he's covered his mouth. He freezes, his eyes wide.

Paul's head shoots up, and he frowns at the door. "Who's there?"

My friends and I exchange an *uh-oh* look. Quickly and quietly, we tiptoe away. Only when we get to the stairwell do we bolt to the ground level. On the way, we come upon Vee walking up as we're sprinting down.

"Whoa!" Vee cries, pressing her body against the stairwell wall to let us pass. "Where are *you* going in such a hurry?"

"Hi, Vee!" I say in a rush. "And...*bye*, Vee!"

Vee looks at us in confusion as we scamper away.

My heart pounds hard as we tumble back onto the pavement. We all lean over our legs to catch our breath.

"Way to blow our cover, Cody," Aubrey grumbles.

Cody holds up his hands. "There's lots of dust in the props room. I'm sensitive!"

Then Aubrey looks at me. "So, is this case number two for the Silver Screen Sleuthios?"

"The *who*?" I ask.

Aubrey grins. "It's our name! I just made it up. Silver Screen Studios, Silver Screen *Sleuth*ios!"

I laugh half-heartedly, but I'm more focused on Aubrey's question. *Is* this a new mystery? I enjoyed solving the case of the ghost, but maybe Paul's right—we should keep our heads down and concentrate on the show.

On the other hand, what if there really *is* a jewel thief? I stare down at my Sadie ring. I wouldn't want *it* to go missing. And I hate the idea of more trouble on the set.

"Maybe," I decide. "Under one condition. We *have* to change our name."

CHAPTER THREE

THE REST OF THAT MORNING, MY FRIENDS AND I SHOOT OUR
first scene of the new episode. It's a school scene—Sadie,
Kiki, and Markus are in geometry when grumpy Principal
Stein, played by an even grumpier woman named Wendy
Bongiovanni, appears in the doorway and says Sadie and
her friends need to come to her office. A video message has
arrived for them from a woman named Princess Stella. She
says she's heard Sadie and her friends are good at solving
mysteries, and she *needs their help*. Sadie and her friends are

to meet her at the gates of her country's embassy the following day at 3:00 p.m.

The crew is tense. This scene is at the beginning of the episode, so this will be the first time the audience meets Princess Stella. And what's the best way to tell an audience that a princess is a princess? *A crown.* Brooklyn Bates shot some later scenes already—and she was wearing the crown that's gone missing. But she hasn't yet recorded this video message to Sadie and her crew. That's not so unusual—TV shows are shot out of order all the time. Brooklyn is scheduled to come back tomorrow and shoot this particular scene, but we're going to need to find her crown by then to make everything match up.

"Maybe we can get another crown?" Paul whispers to Lucinda after our scenes wrap. "Or they can create a replica?"

"The crown is one of a kind," Lucinda says miserably.

"Maybe the princess owns more than one crown?" Paul wonders aloud.

"That seems a little complicated," Lucinda says.

"Guess they haven't found the crown, then," I murmur to Aubrey.

I must say this a little loudly, because Paul turns. "Ladies. Not your concern." Then he snaps his fingers like he has a great idea. "Hey! How would you like to watch *Animals Extraordinaire*?"

"That show about animals doing incredible things?" Cody seems confused. "I thought they hadn't started shooting yet."

Paul smiles. "Today's their first day. I heard it's a lot of fun. There's a kangaroo that can play the piano. And a dog that can do your grocery shopping!" He reaches for his phone. "I'm texting the head animal trainer, Andrew, right now and letting him know you're heading over. You'll have a blast!"

My friends and I share a shrug. "I guess we could go," Aubrey says slowly.

"Sure," I add, trying to stay positive.

But why do I feel like he's trying to get us out of his hair?

♂ ♀

Fifteen minutes later, the three of us are sitting in grandstand-style seats as the live studio audience at *Animals Extraordinaire*. After a border collie finishes racing through *an American Ninja Warrior* style obstacle course, a big Applause sign appears over our heads. *Duh.* Of course we're going to clap for a dog who uses his paws to climb a ladder. And he looked so cute paddling through the swimming part of the course.

"This is fun!" Aubrey says brightly.

Cody lets out another dinosaur-sized sneeze. "*Something* in here is killing my allergies, though."

"I thought you weren't allergic to dogs," Aubrey says.

"I'm not, but there are other animals here."

I scan the other performing animals on the stage. "Armadillos? Kangaroos? Or oh! What if you're allergic to that cute little monkey over there in the tutu? Apparently, she's going to shuffle and deal a deck of cards to a bunch of dogs that can actually play poker later."

"The monkey's a *he*," Cody says, looking at the

program. "His name is Jojo."

"Maybe Cody's allergic to the fact that there's a jewel thief in our midst," Aubrey says.

Cody waves his hand. "There's no jewel thief. We're not in a heist movie."

"How can you be sure?" Aubrey whispers. "Paste is still expensive. Or what if the thief didn't realize the crown wasn't made of real diamonds? What if this person plans to rob a bank next? This is definitely a job for the Silver Screen Sleuthios!"

"We're not calling ourselves the Silver Screen Sleuthios," I groan.

"Besides," Cody adds. "The crown is probably

somewhere on set and Lucinda's just forgotten. I bet it'll turn up by Brooklyn's call time tomorrow."

I cock my head. "Lucinda has an amazing memory when it comes to props, though. Remember our holiday episode last season, when that mastermind hid the stolen charity money inside the toy store? Lucinda had to keep track of every single toy and where it was in the scene. If a Thomas the Tank Engine train moved just a teensy bit out of place, she knew right away and moved it back. If she said she set a crown on her desk, then she set a crown on her desk."

"So what, someone just swooped into the props room and took it away?" Cody asks.

"Yes!" Aubrey chirps. "An international jewel thief! And we'd better stop them, because who knows what they'll steal next!"

A loud snuffle sounds on the stage. The kangaroo has just let out a strange noise because Jojo the monkey has gotten too close.

"Sorry, sorry!" Andrew, says, rushing over. "I think Jojo was curious about what was in Mr. Kang's pouch. This guy loves pockets. I'm thinking of getting him a pair of pants just so he has somewhere to put his hands." He coaxes Jojo to his corner of the set again.

Cody turns back to Aubrey. "How would an international jewel thief even get on the Silver Screen Studios lot? Have you forgotten that ultra-top-secret movie they're filming here? My moms can't even get on the lot without going through like seven security checks."

"Which, by the way, we still need to find out which big actor is in the film," I remind Aubrey, hopefully to distract her from the missing jewels. When we were investigating the ghost thing, a security guard told us that very few guests were being allowed into Silver Screen Studios right now because a very, very famous actor was shooting a movie on the lot. We still haven't figured out *which* actor, though—or where. We keep taking golf cart rides around Silver Screen Studios, thinking we'll spy something top secret, but the only interesting thing we've seen is a guy in a dinosaur costume eating lunch outside the commissary.

"Okay, fine, so it isn't an outsider," Aubrey says. "Someone on our team did it, then."

"Someone from *Sadie Solves It*? No way." I stand by what I told Imogen in the interview. Everyone who works on *Sadie Solves It* is good, honest, and nice. No one would steal.

The lights dim. It's time for the next animal act, a falcon named Julio who can type on a typewriter. Handler Andrew marches on the scene with Julio perched on his arm. He explains what Julio's about to do, adding, "You'll also be thrilled to learn that Julio is an excellent speller!"

We're instructed to applaud again, and everyone does, including Jojo the monkey. Jojo really gets into it, jumping up and down in his sparkly tutu. What a ham.

Next, Handler Andrew wheels out an antique typewriter on a stand. It reminds me of a typewriter prop Sadie used in season 1 in an episode where she was temporarily interning in a newsroom. Where had I seen that type-writer recently?

Then I realize: the props storage room. That's not the new props room, where Lucinda is working on acquiring props for this season. It's another room inside the sound-stage specifically for old props we aren't using anymore. Like the typewriter. And a bunch of old signs. And Sadie's old necklace.

Suddenly, I sit up straighter and turn to my friends. "I think I've got a theory."

CHAPTER FOUR

I'M NERVOUS WHEN I GET BACK TO SET, ESPECIALLY WHEN I
spy Amelia's mom at Stage Five. Mrs. Hart is sitting in
her usual front spot at Video Village, a cluster of monitors inside the soundstage. The monitors are dark right
now, though. Mrs. Hart is alone, her spine very straight, a
determined expression on her face. She reminds me of an
eager student on the first day of school, waiting for classes
to start.

I hide behind a wooden beam. Mrs. Hart always
asks me questions when we run into each other. I don't

know if it's because I'm the lead of the show and she not so secretly wishes her daughter was instead, or maybe it's because Amelia looks up to me and really wants to be good friends. Still, I'd rather avoid Mrs. Hart right now, especially because the person I actually need to talk to is her daughter.

"Hayley?" calls a different voice.

I turn around and see Vee and a young girl who looks like a clone of Vee—light hair, a heart-shaped face.

"I want to introduce you to my daughter Ava," Vee says. "She's a huge fan."

"Hey, Ava," I say.

Vee turns to Ava and starts speaking to her with her hands. It doesn't take me long to understand what she's doing—sign language. I've never seen sign language up close. It's so cool to watch!

"Hey," Ava says to me. She speaks slowly but clearly. "I love the show. And I love the new set."

"Thanks!" I say. Ava nods, able to read my lips.

"Ava wanted to check out the place before she goes into surgery next week," Vee says. "She's getting a cochlear implant!"

"What's that?" I ask.

"Something the doctor will put in her ears to help her hear," Vee answers. "It's going to be great, huh, Ava?"

"I'm really excited," Ava admits.

"That's amazing!" I cry.

Vee says that she's going to take Ava on a golf cart tour around the back lot. I wave goodbye, feeling the normal rush of happiness I always get when I see Vee. She seems like a really good mom.

But now it's time to talk to Amelia. Thankfully, Mrs. Hart didn't seem to overhear my conversation with Vee and Ava, so I head toward Amelia's dressing room in peace. Amelia's room is inside the soundstage. Some of us have trailers outside, others have dressing rooms inside—it's just luck of the draw. I'm just happy her mother isn't in there with her. Usually lunch is Amelia and Mrs. Hart's "mom-and-daughter time."

I think about the theory I voiced to my friends at *Animals Extraordinaire*—is it possible Amelia is behind this? My friends weren't so sure. I hate to suspect Amelia as the thief, but a few weeks ago she'd confessed to swiping the necklace I used to wear in *Sadie* from the old props room. Is it out of the question to think she stole the crown too? I have to ask.

Amelia's dressing room is in the corner of the stage near craft services. The room is on the smallish side, which

I'm sure annoys her—Amelia is forever insisting that she needs the best of everything.

I knock. From inside, I can hear Amelia mumbling softly. *Cooing*, actually. I wonder what that's all about.

I knock again. "Amelia? You in there? It's Hayley."

The door whips open, and at first I don't quite understand what I'm seeing. Amelia is dressed in her Pepper outfit: a rainbow-striped shirt, white overalls, and pink high-tops. Her hair is in two French braids down her back. But there's something unexpected on her shoulder. It's...*scaly*.

"Is that a mini dinosaur?" I blurt out.

Amelia looks at the reptile and smiles. "It's a bearded dragon! I just picked her up from the pet store. She's a perfect pet because of my allergies, you know."

I smirk. Amelia always claims that the reason she stays away from Salmon is because she's allergic, but I suspect she's sort of afraid of him.

I peer at the lizard. He's actually kind of cute. His tiny

hands cling to Amelia's shoulder, and the corners of his mouth stretch in such a way that it looks like he's smiling.

"What's his name?" I ask.

"*Her* name is Thena—short for *Athena*. You know, the goddess of wisdom? Doesn't she look wise?"

"Sure," I say, though I'm not sure the lizard has blinked since I've come in.

I clear my throat. Time to get down to business. I point at Sadie's old necklace, which Amelia is proudly wearing at her throat. "That looks nice on you. But you'll probably have to take it off on set. They made me stop wearing it because it made too much noise."

"Right." Amelia rubs the necklace's delicate chain between her fingers. "I'm only wearing it because Thena really likes the feel of it on her feet." She chuckles. "My mom totally didn't want me to get her. She's kind of mad at me right now! I told her that Thena and I were soul mates the moment I stepped into the pet store, but she just didn't understand."

Aha. That explains why Mrs. Hart was sitting in Video Village by herself.

"I'm sure your mom will come around," I say. "So I was wondering—I don't want you to take this the wrong way, but you don't know anything about the missing crown, do you?"

Amelia's eyes widen. "The princess's crown that went missing off Lucinda's desk? Why would I know anything about that?"

Careful, Hayley. "Well, you did take that necklace from the props room a while back. Maybe you just wanted to try the crown on? I just don't want any more trouble on the set, Amelia. I'm sure you understand."

Two red splotches appear on Amelia's cheeks. "You think *I* took the crown, Hayley?"

"I'm sure you didn't mean to. But if you did take it, and if you're feeling embarrassed about coming forward, we could work something out. I could say I found it, maybe? I'd never have to mention your name." I cough nervously.

"I saw you look guiltily at your backpack when we made that joke about Imogen searching our stuff, Amelia. And as soon as Lucinda ran out of the soundstage saying the crown was missing, you vanished."

Amelia's mouth hangs open. "Okay, first of all, no one was using your necklace anymore. It was in a dusty old box in a storage room, and I didn't think anyone would miss it. I know the difference between an old prop and one that's going to be on this week's episode. And secondly—I can't believe you'd accuse me! I thought we were friends! I looked at my backpack when you made that joke because I had a bunch of books about bearded dragons in there, and I wanted Thena to be a surprise for everyone. And I disappeared before Lucinda ran out because I wanted to go to Julie's Pets down the street to pick Thena up." She glares at me. "Do you believe *that*, or do you want to see the receipt? It's probably time-stamped, just to show you I'm not a liar."

"Okay, okay, never mind," I say, feeling embarrassed. I really stepped into a mess. "I was just making sure."

She puts her hands on her hips. "Did you have to *make sure* with Cody? Or Aubrey?"

"Well, no..."

"Yeah, because they're your real friends!" Her eyes glimmer with tears. "You'd never treat them that way!"

I shut my eyes, feeling deeply regretful. Amelia is right. I should have trusted her. "I'm really sorry. I wasn't thinking, and I hate more gossip on the set, and..."

Amelia waves a hand. Her eyebrows knit together. Even her bearded dragon seems annoyed, his neck frill puffed out. "You need to leave, Hayley. Right now."

"Amelia," I try, "it's not—"

"Right now," she repeats, and then points to the hall. "And to think, I was going to make you Thena's godmother!"

With a sob, she slams the door in my face.

CHAPTER FIVE

I STAND OUTSIDE AMELIA'S DRESSING ROOM, FEELING TERRIBLE. I shouldn't have been so hard on her. Yes, she's needy and annoying and talks way too much about astrology and Greek mythology, but she's younger than I am and eager to be friends. It wasn't right of me to think she'd steal something we need for this episode. I have to get it out of my head that Amelia is trying to sabotage *Sadie Solves It* just because she isn't the star.

I can hear Amelia sniffling. I want to apologize again,

but I doubt Amelia will want to talk to me. Maybe it's better to give her some space.

I wander around Stage Five for a little bit, picking at the offerings at the craft services table and glancing at my scene for this afternoon. It's a scene with me, Cody, and Aubrey, but I keep reading the same sentence over and over. I can't concentrate.

I can't stand it when people are mad at me. And usually, I have good judgment about people. I shouldn't have accused Amelia in the first place.

Slam. A door closes noisily. Amelia is walking toward one of Stage Five's exits. She has the bearded dragon on a leash. I almost burst out laughing, but then I remember how sensitive Amelia is. I want to get back on her good side, not make things worse.

"Amelia!" I run to catch up to her. "Wait!"

Amelia glances over her shoulder and jerks the leash harder. "Come along, Thena. We don't need to talk to *her*."

"I'm sorry," I say. "I don't know what I was thinking. You're totally right—that was not something a good friend should do. And...we *are* friends. I'm serious."

Amelia stops and eyes me carefully. "You mean that?"

"Of course." And I realize I really do. I don't want to lose Amelia as a friend.

"I'm so sorry," I say again. "I shouldn't have accused you of stealing the crown."

Amelia fiddles with the leash handle. I notice that the leash is pink, and Thena's harness is studded with tiny jewels.

"The thing is," Amelia says, "who *did* steal it?"

"I have no idea."

"But you're going to figure it out, right? That's why you asked me? This is your next mystery?"

I shake my head. "I'm done solving mysteries—look at how I just accused you! Obviously my instincts are off. We should leave the sleuthing to Sadie and Pepper."

Amelia pouts. "Are you just telling me that because

you don't want me to help? I really want to be part of the crime-solving team."

"Amelia, there *is* no crime-solving team." I think about Aubrey's awful name for us: *the Silver Screen Sleuthios*. If Amelia found out *that*, she'd never let it go. "As much as I want to know what happened to the crown, Paul won't be happy if we get involved."

"Oh." Amelia's eyes dim. "That's too bad. Solving that ghost stuff was fun."

"I know, but it's for the best." I shift my weight from one foot to another. "You still forgive me though, right?"

"I guess." Then Amelia glances down at Thena, who is in a weird lizard freeze-pose, her squat legs frozen, her head turned like she's sensed danger, and her eyes wide. I *still* haven't seen her blink. "Thena? What is it?"

Suddenly, there's a bloodcurdling scream coming from the other side of the soundstage. A person runs past. It's Amelia's mother herself, white as a sheet. Oh no. What *now*?

"Mom?" Amelia cries, dropping Thena's leash and reaching for her. "Are you okay?" I pick up the leash so the lizard doesn't run away.

Mrs. Hart looks frantically back and forth. "Where's Paul?"

"Probably still at lunch," I report. "What's going on?"

That's when I notice that Amelia's mother is holding her oversized purse in both hands. The bag gapes open, and some of the lining is sticking out like she's been rooting through it all the way to the bottom.

"I've searched and searched," she says in a daze. "My brand-new one-of-a-kind ruby earrings were in here, I just know it. But now *they're missing.*"

CHAPTER SIX

"ANYONE UP FOR TRYING SOMETHING DARING TONIGHT?"
Aubrey is studying the online menu for our favorite pizza
delivery place with a crafty expression. "How about...a
white pie with..." She grins. "Banana peppers and crab?"

"How about *no*," Cody says quickly, making a puking
noise.

"Yeah, Aubrey, that sounds disgusting," I admit.
"Crab doesn't belong on pizza."

Aubrey throws herself onto the couch in mock disap-
pointment. "Just trying to spice things up around here, *jeez*."

"Spice is overrated," Cody declares as Salmon winds his way around his ankles. It's unusual that Salmon is all the way in our secret tree house lair with us, but I'd brought him up the stairs when we came up here immediately after work. The tree house is in my backyard, so I guess it isn't technically a *lair*, but it's the official place where my friends talk about really important things, really *un*important things, and eat a lot of pizza. The delivery guy knows to bring it right to the tree house, not to my family's front door.

"Besides, I think today was plenty spicy," I add, scratching Salmon's ears.

My friends groan in agreement. We're all thinking about Mrs. Hart's missing ruby earrings. One minute they were in her purse, and the next, they were gone. No one had any leads, and no one had seen anyone doing anything suspicious. I remember seeing Mrs. Hart all alone in Video Village, probably escaping Amelia's new lizard—no one was near her. We scoured the soundstage floor, the pavement outside the offices, even Amelia's trailer, thinking maybe the earrings had accidentally fallen out, but they were gone.

Another piece of missing jewelry. I don't like this trend.

"Fine, we'll just get our regular boring pizza," Aubrey grumbles, tapping out our toppings on the order screen. Once we get a confirmation that the pie is on its way, she looks at me curiously. "So, Hayley...what's our first step in figuring out who this jewel thief is?"

I shake my head. "There is no first step. The Silver Screen Sleuthios aren't solving this one."

Aubrey grins. "So you *do* like my name!"

"No, I don't," I grin back. "But since we don't have another name, it's what I have to go with for now. I don't think we should get involved."

"Why not?" Aubrey sticks out her lip in a pout.

I shrug. I'd told them about how terrible I'd felt when I'd accused Amelia. But more than that, I have no idea how to catch a jewel thief or even why someone would want to steal jewels in the first place. I also don't want to think that whoever is doing this is someone involved with *Sadie Solves It.* We've already figured out that it has to be a regular employee at Silver Screen Studios. Now that an item has gone missing from inside *our* soundstage, it seems even more likely that it's someone who works on the show. Unless some random bandit is sneaking onto all the Silver Studios soundstages and rooting through people's purses?

I shut my eyes. "It's just too complicated."

"I'm with Hayley," Cody says. "We should leave this to the experts. And actually, I think it's all just a big misunderstanding."

Aubrey cocks her head. "So you think the earrings are just misplaced? The crown too?"

"Maybe?" Cody sounds hopeful. "All I know is, I need to concentrate on acting so we get to stay in LA. *Not* being a detective."

"Subject change," I announce, clapping my hands. I turn to Aubrey. "Here's a mystery *I* want to solve. Are you going to try out for *Sing Your Heart?*"

A slight smile flickers across Aubrey's face, but then she shrugs. I can tell she doesn't like being in the hot seat, but someone needs to push her about her singing career. Aubrey has so much talent, but for some reason, she's too scared to sing in front of anyone except for me, Cody, and her mom.

But a big audition is coming up. They're making *Sing*

Your Heart, which was a big musical hit on Broadway, into a movie. This is Aubrey's chance.

"I don't know," Aubrey mutters. "The audition is all the way in Tarzana."

"Which is, like, what, a forty-five-minute drive?" I scoff. Tarzana is a suburb of Los Angeles. "It's not like it's at the North Pole."

"Yeah, but my brother has soccer that day," Aubrey adds. "He's on a traveling team too, and he can't miss a practice."

I cross my arms over my chest. "You don't even know which day auditions *are* yet."

"And one of my moms will give you a ride if your parents can't," Cody jumps in.

"Or we'll pay for a taxi," I add.

"I'm not allowed to go in taxis by myself," Aubrey says.

"We'll go with you!" Cody and I say together in voices so forceful they make Aubrey jump back just a little. We giggle.

"You have to audition, Aubrey," I say softly. "You'd be so perfect."

Aubrey picks at an imaginary thread on the couch. "My agent says the same thing. I just... It's too..." She trails off, waving a hand.

"Too scary?" I ask.

"Too important?" Cody says.

"Are you afraid you *will* get the part?" I joke. "Maybe you don't *want* to be a superstar singer?"

"What if my voice cracks?" Aubrey blurts. "Or...or what if I hit the wrong notes? What if I sing the wrong words? What if—oh my God—what if it's a dance number, and I trip over my feet and knock over the whole line of dancers?"

We burst out laughing. But I also feel sad. I hate seeing Aubrey second-guess herself. She's the kind of person who can march up to even the most famous celebrity on the Silver Screen Studios lot and ask for a selfie. She rides every enormous roller coaster at Six Flags

Magic Mountain. She wanted us to investigate the ghost because she thought meeting a ghost would be cool.

"Even if those things happen, *Sing Your Heart* would be lucky to have you," I tell her. "Promise us you'll at least consider trying out?"

Aubrey's shoulders fall. "Fine." Then she wags her fingers at us. "*But*, if at the audition, I try to sing a note and a burp comes out? Or if they make me do a high kick and I split my pants? *Or* if I get so into my singing that I wave my hand and knock over a set wall? I'll say I told you so. And it'll be all your fault."

"I'm totally prepared to take the blame," I tell her.

And believe me, I would be.

CHAPTER SEVEN

IT'S CLOUDY THE NEXT MORNING, WHICH IS UNUSUAL FOR LA. There's also a lot of traffic on the freeway, and we're stuck in a jam for over an hour. I shift in the back seat, worrying I'm going to miss my call time. That's the time you're supposed to be on set to give hair, makeup, and wardrobe enough time to get you ready. Worst of all, my dad is listening to the local radio station as he drives, and between songs, the DJs use this annoying air horn sound that keeps startling me.

"Can you change the channel, Dad?" I whine.

Salmon must agree, because he bumps up against the front of his cat carrier and meows noisily.

My dad glances at me in the rearview. "But these DJs are funny. Haven't you been listening to their jokes?"

The station breaks for commercial, and I'm surprised when an ad for *Animals Extraordinaire* comes on. *"New episode tonight!"* an announcer says. *"You won't believe what Jojo the monkey is going to show our audience! We'll give you a hint—he's a bit of a card shark!"*

I bark out a laugh. "That's the show shooting right next to us. Cody, Aubrey, and I watched them record that episode."

"Does the monkey really play cards?" my dad asks.

"No, he's just the dealer," I recall, thinking of the nimble monkey passing out playing cards to the table full of terrier dogs. It was pretty amazing, actually. The monkey shuffled better than someone who works in Las Vegas.

Finally, the traffic breaks, and we pull into Silver Screen Studios. Timothy, the head security guard at the gate, checks our credentials.

"Any news on that top secret movie they're filming?" I ask him.

Timothy leans in closer. "You didn't hear it from me, but I'd check out Stage Twenty-one if I were you."

I flash him a smile. *Stage Twenty-one!* Aubrey will love this hot tip. She loves celebrity spotting.

My dad gives me a kiss before I climb out of the car. Unlike Amelia's mom, my parents don't always stay with me on the set—we have a tutor, Miss Rose, who helps us with schoolwork, and the PAs act as chaperones too.

I head to my trailer and fling open the door. The first thing I notice is that it smells a little like something familiar. A candy bar? Or maybe...peanut butter. I smile. I *love* peanut butter.

Someone has placed today's lines on my couch. I grab them eagerly, excited to see if I have any scenes with Brooklyn Bates, Princess Stella. Sure enough, I do! It looks like Sadie and Markus, Cody's character, are going through town hall records to see who adopted the princess's long-lost twin sister—according to the Princess's message to Sadie and her crew, she's traced her long-lost twin to Sadie's town, but she doesn't know who she is.

Just as Sadie finds some files, the lights go out. It's really spooky. They think someone is chasing them through the courthouse. Maybe someone who doesn't want Sadie and her friends digging into this secret.

I fly through the pages eagerly. It's a really fun scene. When I finish, I place the pages on my couch and go to stand.

Then I see it.

There's a little side table next to my couch where I put the TV remote, a can of soda, and sometimes a box of tissues. But today, there's two extra items sitting on the table too. A pair of earrings that aren't mine.

A pair of *ruby* earrings.

♂ ♀

"Hayley, calm down," Paul says, walking around to comfort me as soon as I walk into the room. I'm in tears. Mrs. Hart's ruby earrings are in my trembling palms. "We'll figure this out."

"I didn't steal them. I *swear*. I have no idea what they were doing in my trailer."

"We know you didn't steal them," Paul assures me. "Mrs. Hart won't accuse you either. She'll be happy to know they're back, that's all."

I think of how I accused Amelia of stealing the crown. It looks bad that her mom's earrings have suddenly

shown up in *my* trailer. I want an explanation about how they got there.

"Do you think someone planted them?" I pause to sniffle. "Do you think someone is trying to blame it on me?"

Paul's mouth twists. "I'd hate to think someone would do that." But then he pauses. "Though we might be able to see what *did* happen."

He turns to his computer monitor. "After the whole ghost problem, we installed extra cameras around the set—just to make sure that if there *was* another mystery, we wouldn't have to trouble our stars trying to solve it." He shoots me a pointed look, then wiggles the computer mouse. "A few of the cameras are placed outside with a view of the trailers. I barely look at them because I don't like invading people's privacy. And the video footage erases after twenty-four hours."

"But maybe we'll see something on the footage," I say eagerly. "Amelia's mom's earrings only went *missing* twenty-four hours ago. And when I left my trailer last night, the earrings definitely weren't there."

Then I get a twinge of embarrassment. I had no idea cameras are set up outside our trailers. Just last week, I'd stood in the corridor between the trailers with my phone outstretched, trying to imitate this dance I liked on TikTok. The dance was hard, though, with a lot of parts, and at one point I tripped over my feet and fell flat on my butt. Hopefully *that* vanished from the video feed before anyone saw it.

"Let's see what we got," Paul says, clicking into the app on his computer. He scrolls past a series of black-and-white video feeds. One is the stairwell in the offices. Another is of the ramp leading into the soundstage. He finds a view that includes my trailer—I know it's mine because I have the cutest fan art of Salmon hanging up on the door.

"We'll rewind to yesterday," Paul says, clicking some more.

He hits play. We watch the screen. Not much happens. The time stamp says it's past 6:00 p.m.—my friends and I were already gone for the day. We watch fifteen seconds of nothing but a view of my trailer door. Paul hits the fast-forward button. For a long time, the image on the screen doesn't change. The shadows grow longer. The sky grows dark. The streetlights snap on. Car headlights illuminate the door and then fade.

In the corner of the screen, I see 1:00 a.m. roll by, and then 2:00. I watch all the way to 7:00, which isn't much earlier than when I arrived on set today. That's when I see a blip appear in fast-forward, popping on the screen and disappearing.

"Wait!" I cry. "Pause it! Someone was there!"

Paul stops the fast-forward and then rewinds until the figure comes into view. I suck in a breath. The person's head is down, and they're carrying a large messenger-style bag. I watch as they look back and forth carefully, and then sneak into my trailer. The door bangs shut.

I put a hand to my mouth. Someone *did* plant the earrings. I can't believe it!

"Who was that?" Paul says, leaning closer to the screen. "Do we know them?"

I'm not sure either. The person's head was down when they went into my trailer. But when they leave, for a brief moment, their chin is raised, and I can get a good look at her face.

Paul hits Pause. A crushed expression comes over his features. "Is that..." he asks.

My heart is sinking too. The woman's face is petite and heart-shaped. Her eyes are gentle and kind. But her shoulders are hunched like she feels guilty about something. She looks around nervously like she's about to get in trouble.

It's my favorite person on the set. The makeup artist, *Vee*.

CHAPTER EIGHT

"PAUL, THIS HAS GOT TO BE A MISTAKE," I BEG.

It's a half hour later. We're standing outside the soundstage next to a golf cart marked SILVER STUDIOS SECURITY. Two guards have gone inside the makeup trailer, and I watch helplessly as they walk out with Vee. She's got handcuffs on her wrists and there's a baffled look on her face. My gut twists. I feel like this is all my fault.

I look at Paul, who's standing next to me, Aubrey, and Cody. "We don't have to do this, do we?" I beg. "Vee

wouldn't take the earrings. They aren't even her style."
Vee is more into big, flashy hoops than fancy rubies.

Paul lets out a long sigh. "I know. But because this is
the second instance of theft and Vee is the only person who
went into your trailer—*and* because Mrs. Hart reported the
earrings missing to security, we have to follow the rules."

"What are the rules?" Aubrey looks nervous. "Vee
isn't going to jail, is she?"

Paul shakes his head. "No, but security needs to
investigate. For now, Vee can't work here."

"Paul, no!" I gasp. "Vee needs this job. Her daughter
is having surgery on her ears next week. How can she pay
for it if she doesn't work here?"

Paul looks down sadly. "My hands are tied, Hayley.
I'm sorry."

I can feel tears in my eyes. Vee doesn't deserve this.
Neither does Ava.

Security heads toward us. I gulp back a lump in my
throat as Vee passes. She stops and gives me a weak little smile.

"Vee," I cry. "I'm so sorry. I know this is a huge mistake."

"It's okay," Vee says. "If I had earrings that went missing and someone looked suspicious, I'd want someone to investigate every angle too."

It hurts even more that Vee is being so nice. She isn't blaming me. She doesn't even seem mad.

"But...what *were* you doing in my trailer?" I whisper.

"Dropping off your script," Vee answers. "The other PAs were tied up, and Amanda asked me if I could run if over."

My mouth drops open. "Have you told someone that? Has Amanda?"

"Of course." She shrugs. "But it doesn't matter. I *could* have had the earrings too. Not that I did—I'm just saying." Then she clutches my hands. "You know I'd never frame you, right?"

"Of course," I answer. Then I clear my throat. "What about Ava? The surgery?"

Vee's smile dims. "We might have to postpone it.

I'm not really looking forward to telling Ava, but she'll be okay."

Tears are running down my cheeks. This all feels so wrong! I don't want Vee to be blamed. I don't want her to have to go home without pay or for Ava to have to wait for her surgery. Someone else put those earrings in my trailer. *Obviously.* Only, how did they avoid the video cameras? Is it someone who's skilled at tech stuff and managed to shut the cameras down for a little while so we don't have the footage? Or maybe someone climbed through my trailer's back window and wasn't even *on* the camera?

I bolt up. That's it!

I turn to Paul. "My trailer has a window. I think I left it open. That's how someone could have climbed in and left the earrings!"

Paul frowns and rubs his chin. "Huh," he says. "You really think so?"

"I do. We just have to figure out who squeezed through and left those earrings there."

He narrows his eyes. "I don't want you getting involved in this stuff again, Hayley." Then he gestures to Vee and the security guards, who are now heading toward the front entrance. "Leave the investigation to the experts. They'll figure out what's really going on."

I nod like I agree, but it's not what I'm feeling inside. I *have* to get involved now. I need to clear Vee's name. Ava deserves to have the surgery. Someone climbed through my trailer window, and that's the jewel thief, I just *know* it.

Aubrey is still standing next to me, and she must sense a change in my energy, because she eyes me curiously. Then, the corners of her mouth curl into a sly smile. "Are you thinking what I'm thinking?" she murmurs. "Do the Silver Screen Sleuthios have a case?"

"The Silver Screen Sleuthios have a case," I admit.

And then I burst out laughing. I just said *Silver Screen Sleuthios*.

Guess that's our name now whether I like it or not.

CHAPTER NINE

TEN MINUTES LATER, CODY, AUBREY, AND I ARE SITTING ON the front porch of Sadie's TV house. It's not really a house at all—the structure looks like a house, but it's actually just a front of a building with a great deck and pretty front door. Inside, there aren't even any real rooms—we shoot all of the interior scenes on Stage Five.

But the back lot is private. The other shows shooting right now either aren't back here today or everyone is at lunch. Private is exactly what we need in order to discuss our top-secret business.

"So I've already checked," Aubrey says, frowning at something on her phone. "There are no cameras near your trailer's back window, Hayley. So we can't see if someone snuck in that way. But we can still think through what might have happened."

"Right," I say. "Okay. What could someone's motive be for stealing jewelry in the first place?"

"Money?" Aubrey suggests. "First a crown with what looks like real diamonds goes missing. Then ruby earrings. Maybe someone wants to sell them."

"Maybe," Cody echoes. "Do we know anyone who needs money?"

I can think of lots of people who've mentioned they're saving up for things. Tina, who works in craft services, is always talking about how someday she wants to buy a speedboat. I overheard some of the production assistants talking about saving for a group trip to Hawaii. Even Vee told me the other day she'd just been hit with a big veterinary bill after her golden retriever, Rex, who loves to eat everything in sight, swallowed a pair of nail clippers.

But just because Vee said that doesn't mean she's guilty.

"Vee didn't do this," I repeat to my friends, ashamed I even thought such a thing. "Absolutely no way."

"Of course she didn't," Aubrey echoes. "This one time, when Vee was doing my makeup so it looked like I had a black eye, I was running so late that I hurried out of there without grabbing my Nintendo Switch. Vee ran after me, giving it back immediately, even though I'd been telling her all about how I'd gotten a sneak-peek early copy of the new *Animal Crossing* game. Did you know she's wild about *Animal Crossing*? I wouldn't have been mad if she would have kept the Switch for a little bit, maybe fiddled around with the game just to see what it looked like. But she didn't. She returned it straight to me."

"We all have stories like that about Vee. She installed a cat door in her trailer for Salmon! She loves us!" I rock back and forth on one of the four rocking chairs on Sadie's family's front porch. "Also, she wouldn't do anything to risk her job with Ava's ear surgery coming up."

"I don't think it was her either," says a voice.

My head whips up, and I tense, worried someone is spying on us. Paul doesn't want us to be trying to solve this case, and he might get mad if he finds out we're talking about this instead of learning our lines.

But it's Amelia who stands in the street, hands on her hips, a disappointed look on her face. She has her new bearded dragon, Thena, on the leash again.

Aubrey squints at the reptile curiously. "What *is* that thing?"

"It's a bearded dragon," Amelia says in a frosty voice. "Her name is Thena."

"May I pet it?" Aubrey asks.

"I don't think so. Thena is very picky about who touches her." Then she looks at me. "Hayley. You promised I could be part of the investigation."

"Whoa, whoa, whoa." I raise my hands in surrender. "There isn't an investigation yet."

Amelia looks between us. "But that's what you all are talking about, right? That Vee didn't do it?" When we don't answer, she takes this as a yes, picks up the lizard, and climbs up the steps to the porch, settling into the fourth rocking chair. Thena sits in her lap not unlike Salmon often nestles in mine.

"I want to help," Amelia declares.

Cody shoots me a look, but I shrug. "She's right,"

I tell my friends. "When I apologized for accusing her of stealing the crown, she asked to be part of solving the mystery."

"And I can be helpful," Amelia boasts. "Considering it's my mother's earrings that went missing."

"Okay, let's talk about that," Aubrey challenges. I can tell she's still miffed that Amelia didn't let her pet her dragon. "What can you tell us about your mom's earrings?"

"Well, they were very expensive," Amelia says. "My dad gave them to her on their twentieth wedding anniversary. He had them made especially for her. That's why she was so upset—it's not like she could just go to a jewelry store and replace them."

"Huh." I rub my chin. "Had your mom talked about the earrings to a lot of people? Like, that they were a gift, and where your dad got them?" I have a feeling Mrs. Hart did. She talks to anyone who will listen, and a lot of what she says is kind of a brag. Maybe her name-dropping an expensive jewelry store caught someone's attention. Especially someone who needed some money.

Of course, that would mean someone on the set is guilty. I hate the idea that someone we work with could be a suspect. And after the mistake I made with Amelia, I definitely don't want to make random accusations.

"Here's the thing, though," Amelia says, breaking through my thoughts. She's stroking Thena's scaly head as she speaks. "Even if someone was impressed by how much the earrings cost, they didn't sell them, in the end."

"That's true," Aubrey says. "They planted them. In Hayley's trailer."

Amelia sits back and thinks. "So maybe it's someone who has something against *you*, Hayley."

"Me?" I cry. "Why would someone have something against me?" I try to think if there's anyone who might be mad at me. Amelia was before, but that's settled now.

"Or what if the person was going to sell them but then chickened out?" I suggest. "Maybe my trailer was close and easy. And I left the window open. They snuck through."

"It's a thought," Cody says. "*Or*, there's also the fact that Vee was the only person who went into your trailer that morning. Maybe whoever took the earrings knows that—and maybe it was more that they wanted to frame Vee."

"But everyone loves Vee," I argue.

"Are we sure?" Aubrey says. "I mean, *we* love Vee, but maybe we should ask her."

I cross my arms. Maybe she's right.

I'm about to say this when I hear the near-silent *whirr* of a golf cart. I stiffen, worried once again it's Paul.

Instead, Andrew the trainer from *Animals Extraordinaire* sits in the driver's seat. He's got the performing kangaroo in his lap, and the kangaroo is resting his paws on the steering wheel, actually steering the thing. Lounging next to him, like all of this is totally normal, is Jojo, the monkey in the tutu. Sitting in the back is one of the dogs that played poker.

Andrew notices us and waves. Jojo the monkey does too. I get a whiff of the monkey's fur. He smells like the zoo. That guy should really think of slapping on cologne! Then, the kangaroo wildly steers them past, first nearly crashing into the curb, and then almost taking out a fake mailbox.

Now *that's* not something you see every day.

CHAPTER TEN

"OKAY, THERE ARE WAY TOO MANY TOPPINGS TO CHOOSE from," Cody says, frowning. "Who wants Nerds on their ice cream? Who wants gummy worms?"

"I happen to like gummy worms on my ice cream," Aubrey says, reaching past him and scooping a spoonful of fluorescent-colored worms into her cup.

We're at Scoops, a make-your-own frozen yogurt place on Hollywood Boulevard. There are tons of tourists streaming past outside, all of them posing for pictures with someone dressed as Godzilla, another person dressed as

Harry Potter, and two people dressed like Superman. We've filled our cups with yummy-sounding flavors— mint Oreo, marshmallow cream, chocolate strawberry explosion—and now it's time for toppings.

Cody, as usual, is analyzing every topping, trying to figure out which one is best. Aubrey, on the other hand, is piling on *every* topping, wanting to try them all. I'm strictly a rainbow sprinkles girl. And Amelia, who's also with us, is eating her fro-yo plain, claiming she has food sensitivities to most of the toppings that are offered.

"Miss?" The teenage girl behind the counter suddenly straightens, looking at Amelia. "Um, you can't have that lizard in here."

Amelia glances at her bearded dragon perched on her shoulder. "She's my emotional support animal."

"Amelia, don't *lie*," I hiss. I grab her cup and take it to the register, smiling sweetly at the worker. "It's okay. We'll eat outside."

The worker doesn't ring us up right away, instead

staring around at all of us. Her mouth drops open. "Wait, you're on that show!" she cries. "*Sadie Solves It!*"

"Guilty as charged," I admit shyly.

It turns out the ice cream employee is a fan, so we all happily take selfies. After that's done, she sadly repeats that the store doesn't allow pets, so we have to leave. It's better that way. A seat outside means we'll be able to see Vee as soon as she arrives. I'm so happy she even agreed to meet us at all.

It's great timing, because moments after we take our seats at a shaded table, Vee strides around a corner, narrowly avoiding a bear hug from a guy dressed up like Bigfoot. Or maybe Chewbacca? I can't tell. It's especially funny because Vee is pretty short, and the Bigfoot guy towers over her.

Vee waves at us, and I'm relieved to see she's her usual friendly self. I blame myself for Vee's troubles. Had I not found those earrings in my trailer, had I not gone to Paul and asked him to review the videos, maybe she would still be doing makeup. She was just in the wrong place at the wrong time.

"Want ice cream?" I ask after we all hug Vee and she sits down.

"Nah, that's okay," Vee says. "Just had dinner. So what's up?"

I stick my spoon into my remaining scoop of strawberry. "First of all, how's Ava?"

Vee smiles. "She's okay. Sad the surgery is delayed, but she's hanging in there."

"We want to fix this," I tell her. "And make sure you get your job back. It just isn't fair!"

Cody explains our idea about the open window at the back of my trailer and how the thief might have crawled in that way. Aubrey jumps in to add that we think it might be someone who either wanted to frame me—or frame *Vee*.

"We've been trying to think through who might want to do that to you or Hayley," Amelia says next. "And

we were wondering if you've had trouble with anyone on the set."

"Me?" Vee runs a hand through her dark hair, and her already big eyes go even wider. "Wow. I didn't think about that." She thinks about this for a minute. "You know, the woman who plays Sadie's principal, Mrs. Stein? She complained about her makeup the other day."

"Wendy Bongiovanni?" I ask. That's the name of the actress.

"Yeah. She said my makeup made her look angry." Vee rolls her eyes. "That was the point, though. Mrs. Stein *is* angry. She's the big, bossy principal. That's how she's described in the script."

Aubrey dabs at her mouth. "Wendy's in this episode a lot. First when Sadie and the others are called into her office for that top secret message from the princess. And I saw her name on the call sheet for later this week too."

I frown. "Do you think Wendy would try and get you fired because she didn't like your makeup job, Vee?"

"I *hope* not," Vee says. Then she gets a far-off look. "I also recently had a little fight with Clem in craft services."

"Clem?" I'm surprised. Clem works with Tina. He's tall, always smiling, and always knows the latest TikTok dances. "What about?"

"He never puts out enough nut-free snacks for everyone who wants them. I'm allergic, and I know some other people on the set are too, but he only puts out a few things labeled nut-free, and runs out of them right away. So I called him out on it. He didn't take it well."

"You were only pointing it out so people didn't get hurt," Aubrey says.

"Yeah, but I spoke loudly," Vee admits. "I think I embarrassed him. I shouldn't have done that. I think he's sensitive."

"Hmm." Now that I think about it, *I'd* kind of upset Clem recently too. Last week, I was devouring the muffins Tina always brings to set, and I noticed Clem watching me, looking disappointed. He was sad I never ate stuff *he* baked, and then he gestured to this weird fruitcake thing on the table. No one had taken a piece. But, I mean, it's *fruitcake*. It looked gross.

Is Clem mad at both of us—and trying to get both of us in trouble? I really don't want to believe that...

"Anyone else?" Amelia asks. Thena has climbed down from her shoulder, and Amelia is feeding her a bite of yogurt. Or, well, putting the spoon to the lizard's lips, but Thena doesn't seem very interested in trying it.

Vee twists her mouth. "I don't think so."

Cody tilts his head like he has an idea. "Paul mentioned we were going to have a substitute makeup artist for the next few days. Does anyone know who it is?"

"Actually, I heard Elizabeth took the job," I pipe up.

"Elizabeth the PA?" Vee gets a strange look on her face. "Huh."

"What?" Cody asks.

Vee shrugs. "Well, she's been hanging around my trailer lately, asking all kinds of questions about how I got the job working on *Sadie*. Apparently, she took a course in makeup and is thinking of getting into the business too."

Amelia widens her eyes. "Do you think Elizabeth stole the jewels because she wanted to get you fired to take your spot as the show's makeup artist?"

"That doesn't sound like something she'd do." Vee shifts uncomfortably. "She's been so nice. I've even given her some pointers and had her practice on this dummy head I have in the trailer. I don't want to think she'd frame me."

At that moment, the hair on my arms starts to prickle. I look around. Tourists pass by. The two Supermans are competing in a dance-off. The Bigfoot is posing for pictures. And yet, I swear someone is staring at us. *Watching.*

Is it the jewel thief?

"It's a start," I say, rising from my chair. Suddenly, I want to be safe at home—or at least in the tree house. I look around at the group. "I guess we have some questions to ask."

CHAPTER ELEVEN

WE SHOOT SOME EXCITING SCENES THE NEXT DAY. BROOKLYN Bates is back on set, and Sadie and her friends are tracking down some leads to figure out who could be her long-lost twin sister. You'd think that would be easy to do, but the twins were separated at birth, with Brooklyn's character leaving with the royal family, and her twin sister vanishing from the hospital.

In the latest scene, Cody, Aubrey, Brooklyn, and I stand on the busy street in Sadie's town, trying to figure it out. Extras pass by us to make it look like it's a bustling day downtown.

"The thing is," I say to Brooklyn as Sadie, "because you weren't identical twins, it's not like we'll recognize your sister. She could be *hiding in plain sight*."

"Cut!" Monique the director shouts.

The extras scatter, and Monique steps toward us, smiling. "Great job, Hayley. I think we nailed it."

"Great job, everyone," Brooklyn gushes. "I'm so impressed with how talented you all are."

I feel a little thrill. It's not every day a mega movie star compliments your acting talent. It's so cool that Brooklyn is so *normal*. She came to work with blueberry muffins for everyone. She squealed when she met Salmon. She's also clumsy, showing us a Band-Aid on her elbow from when she banged it in the shower this morning.

"I wonder who Princess Stella's sister is?" I ask, turning to Brooklyn. "Do *you* know?"

"Nope." Brooklyn unclips her tiny microphone from inside her shirt. "Monique hasn't given me the final pages."

"She never gives them to us, either!" Aubrey cries.

"She says it's because she wants us to be genuinely surprised at the big reveal."

"That's smart," Brooklyn remarks. "Do you guys have any theories?"

I look at some of the series regulars milling around. Caity Howe is here, who plays Sadie's neighbor—maybe her? Or perhaps it's Gilda, who works at Sadie and her friends' favorite pizza shop? On the other hand, our last episode was all about the pizza shop, so maybe not.

Then I notice another woman pass by, her features arranged into a deep scowl. Wendy Bongiovanni, who plays Mrs. Stein, Sadie's principal.

And also maybe the jewel thief? Did she grab those earrings and frame Vee because she was upset at how Vee did her makeup?

I nudge my friends, glancing in Wendy's direction. The actress has stopped next to Monique and is speaking to her in a low voice about something. Monique answers, and then Wendy nods and heads toward her trailer.

"Which one of us is going to question her about Vee and the earrings?" I ask.

"I call dibs on Elizabeth," Aubrey says quickly, naming the PA who's the new makeup artist. "At least she's friendly."

Clem, the guy in craft services, is friendly too," Cody argues. "I'll take him."

"Wait a minute!" I can't believe it. "I didn't volunteer to question Wendy!"

"You're the best person for the job, Hayley," Aubrey assures me. "And the bravest."

"*I'll* go with you," says a voice. And here's Amelia, sliding up to me with her lizard in tow. "We'll question her together."

I have to admit, Amelia coming with me is comforting. Still, I feel uneasy as we walk to the temporary trailer Wendy is using and knock gently on the door. A few moments of silence pass. Reluctantly, I knock again.

"What?" snaps a voice from inside.

Amelia and I exchange a worried glance. I want to run away, but I'm the leader. I muster up all my courage. "Um, Miss Bongiovanni? It's Hayley. You know, I play Sadie?"

The door whips open. Wendy looks at me curiously. "Of course I know who you are. I've only been acting on this show for two seasons." She glances between me and Amelia. "What's going on, girls?"

"Um..." I'm not sure how to start. "How are you?"

Wendy looks puzzled. It's not like we regularly chat. "Stressed, actually. I have a lot of lines to learn. The writers just threw them at me."

Sadie's principal has a lot of lines? That's interesting. "We'll let you get back to that," Amelia says. "We were just, um, taking a poll. How are you feeling now that Vee's gone?"

Wendy blinks. "Vee? Who's Vee?"

"The makeup artist?" I pretend to sweep a big fluffy brush across my cheeks, like I'm applying blush. I probably look ridiculous.

"That's her name?" Wendy asks. "Vee? I thought it was Matilda."

"Yes. She made you look really angry, right? Her last makeup job? You told her that?"

Wendy shrugs, looking more and more confused. "*Did* I? I don't know. I never like how the makeup people make me look. It's always so...overdone. Why the fake eyelashes? Why the dark eyebrows? Why so much lipstick?"

Amelia and I glance at each other again. "So you don't like when *anyone* does your makeup?" I ask.

"Nope. I'd prefer to do my makeup myself. Back when

I was in theater, that's how it was always done," Wendy says loftily.

"And where were you this past Tuesday morning?" Amelia blurts.

I shoot Amelia a warning look. She wasn't supposed to just rush in there with accusations! Wendy might get suspicious!

I say, kindly, "What we mean to say was, there was a beautiful sunrise over the studio Tuesday morning. Were you here to see it?"

Wendy shrugs. "I wasn't here. I wasn't needed that day. Sorry, girls, what's this about? I really need to go back to studying my lines."

Wendy didn't frame Vee, I think. Seems like she hates all makeup artists, not just Vee. And she wasn't even here Tuesday morning.

"All good!" I cry, now just wanting to end our little talk. "Sorry to bother you! We'll go now!"

But suddenly, just before I move to close the door,

Wendy seems to notice something. Her face softens, and she breaks into a smile. A rather *pretty* smile, actually.

"Oh my goodness!" She points to Amelia. "Is that a bearded dragon?"

"Uh, yeah." Amelia pivots to move closer. "I just got her a few days ago."

"I had bearded dragons as a little kid!" Wendy sounds overjoyed. "It was the happiest time of my life!" She starts to talk in a baby voice as she pets Thena's rough, wrinkled little head. *"Aren't you a smoopie poo! Aren't you the cutest widdle dwagon I ever saw! Yes you are! Yes you are!"*

"Thena really likes you," Amelia says. "You can visit her anytime."

"Really?" Wendy cries. She looks so different now. Her eyes are brighter, the frown lines around her mouth are gone... I'm not even afraid of her anymore! Goes to show you—even someone who might *seem* mean might not be, deep down.

After Wendy tickles under Thena's chin, Amelia and I

head back to set. Cody is emerging from Stage Five. Aubrey has just exited from the offices.

"Did you talk to Clem?" I ask them. "And Elizabeth?"

"Yep," Cody says. "Clem didn't do it. You won't believe what he told me—he has a *crush* on Vee. He'd never want her fired."

"And Elizabeth burst into tears when I mentioned Vee's name," Aubrey says. "She's devastated that Vee isn't on set to help her. Vee was teaching her everything she knows. She feels overwhelmed. She's ready to quit!"

"Ooh, I wonder if she's a Cancer," Amelia says. "They are *so* emotional."

I slump down onto a bench, feeling both relieved and frustrated. I'm glad none of those people took the earrings or wanted to frame me or Vee. But at the same time, it means we have no answers. It means Vee is still fired. It means Ava still can't get her surgery.

We need to find the jewel thief.

CHAPTER TWELVE

I'M NOT IN THE AFTERNOON'S SCENES, BUT I WATCH AUBREY, Cody, and Amelia. There's a "B" story in this episode about Pepper, Amelia's character, overcoming her fear of trying mushrooms, a food she's always been afraid of. She entered a pizza-eating contest, with the first prize being free pizza for a year. To win, she has to eat pizza with lots of toppings. Aubrey's character, Kiki, and Cody's character, Markus, are coaxing her to take tiny bites of mushrooms to get used to them for the big contest. I keep cracking up at the funny faces Amelia-as-Pepper makes when they wave the fork in her face. By the way, a "B" story on a show is a smaller situation that's happening at the same time as the main story in the episode. The "B" story is usually pretty light and often funny, like Pepper and her fear of mushrooms. Next time you watch a show, pay careful attention. A lot of shows have "B" stories. Some of them even have "C" stories!

When shooting ends, I head back to my trailer and grab my stuff. As soon as I open the trailer door, I notice that Salmon is acting strangely. His tail is puffed up. It usually only gets like that when he sees a bird he wants to attack or a barking dog. He also doesn't come over to me right away, but instead glances at me with his wide, yellow eyes and lets out a distressed *meow*.

"What is it, Salmon?" I drop to my knees. "Are you sick?"

Salmon looks okay. His eyes are bright, his nose is wet, and I don't see any gashes on his fur. When I offer him one of Aubrey's homemade cat treats, he gobbles it right up. I notice he has some kind of glitter on his tail. I wonder if he accidentally rolled in hairspray or something.

Yet it seems like something spooked him. I look around the trailer, checking to see if anything is out of place. Maybe a bird got in here?

That's when I realize.

I'd taken off my ring after my scene this morning. I'd noticed it was dirty, and I wanted to use this special liquid I had at home to make it sparkly again. I should

have known better. Because now, my precious *Sadie* ring is *gone*.

"Oh no," I moan. "Oh no, oh *no*."

Then I realize something else. If the jewel thief struck again, that means it can't be Vee. She's not here today! I can't wait to tell Paul—now Vee can get her job back and Ava can get her surgery. That's good, anyway.

But my ring! I love my ring. It's one of a kind. Paul and the others were depending on me not to lose it. Which, I mean, I *didn't* lose it—someone took it.

Only...who?

"Hayley?" There's a knock on my trailer door. Aubrey and Cody peek in. "You okay in there?"

I turn to them, biting hard on my lip so that I don't burst into tears. "My ring is gone."

"*What*?" Aubrey scrambles into the trailer. "When? How?"

I explain everything I know. We're all happy that this gets Vee off the hook, but I can't help think about how much I loved that ring. I can't believe someone would take it from me.

We try and talk through how this could have happened. Then Aubrey looks up, her eyes wide. "Wait a minute. You said Salmon was acting weird? What if he *ate* your ring?"

"Salmon didn't eat my ring!" I laugh. "Salmon eats cat treats. Not jewelry."

But then *I* have a thought. I turn back to Salmon. His tail is still a giant puff. He looks like a black raccoon. He's been in this trailer all afternoon, and I took off my ring after lunch. Which means...

"Salmon." I sit down next to him. "You saw who took it. Is that why you're acting so strange?"

Salmon answers with a *meow*.

Aubrey scoots over to Salmon too. "Can you tell us?" she asks my cat excitedly.

"Is it a man or a woman?" I ask. "Did they climb through the window again, or come through the front door?"

I know this is silly. Cats can't talk, not even an amazing cat like Salmon.

I sit back. "I can't believe Salmon saw the jewel thief."

And I *really* can't believe he's not telling us who it is.

CHAPTER THIRTEEN

THE TREES IN THE WOODS ARE THICK AND TWISTED WITH A LOT of branches. A bug lands on my arm, and I yelp and swat it away. My heart is pounding—woods always scare me a little. I know I shouldn't be afraid, as these "woods" are only a few trees, some bushes, and murky pond. But still, it's spooky. I'm always afraid a snake or a spider is lurking under the leaves. Filmmakers use this area for horror scenes. The last time I walked into these woods, I found a fake eyeball sticking to a tree.

I notice her after I take a few more steps forward. A woman sits cross-legged on a tree stump with her eyes closed. Her hands rest softly on her knees.

"Siobhan?" I call out quietly.

Her eyes pop open. "Hayley! Are you here to meditate?"

I hurry forward. Siobhan Cross, an actor on *Sadie,* meditates in these woods every afternoon, so I knew this was where I could find her. I'm never sure about bothering meditating people, though. I worry that breaking their spell is like interrupting a sleepwalker and they'll become really confused.

I crouch down beside her. Siobhan is wearing a flowy dress, a pink headscarf, and a big silver ring on every finger. She plays Madame Curio, Sadie's psychic friend. They couldn't have chosen a better actress to play Madame Curio, actually. Siobhan fully believes in magic, is a little bit mysterious, and claims that she, just like Madame Curio, can see things others can't.

It's why I've come looking for her today.

I take a breath. "I'm having a hard time with something."

Siobhan widens her eyes Madame Curio style. "The thefts, right?"

See? This is why she's the perfect psychic. She can read minds! "Yes!" I say. "Did you hear about the latest one? My ring went missing?"

Siobhan nods sadly. "I'm so sorry to hear that. It's so unfair."

I pull my knees into my chest. "I just can't figure out why it's happening. All of the thefts...they don't link together. I can't figure out who would be doing this, or why. There's no common motive."

A moth flaps past us. I watch it for a moment as it flutters into the trees. "I wish I knew the answer," Siobhan says. "I wish that we could just flip to the end of a *Sadie* script and all would be revealed." But then she gets a wise look on her face like she's thought of something. She turns to me, a playful smile on her face. "Something's behind your ear," she says in a teasing voice.

"What?" I ask, touching my ear.

Siobhan reaches back there too. I watch as she pulls her arm back, wiggles her wrist, and a quarter appears between her fingers. I giggle. My dad used to do that quarter trick with me when I was little.

"You know how that trick works, right?" Siobhan says.

I nod. "You have the quarter hidden in your palm. You just made it seem like you pulled it behind my ear by waving your fingers."

"Exactly." Siobhan's eyes shine. "It's called *sleight of hand*. A magician's secret. I distracted you. Making you believe one thing while I was really doing something else. Maybe that's what's happening with these missing items? Perhaps the thefts don't link together because they're not *supposed* to. Maybe you're looking for patterns when there aren't any."

I cock my head. "So the thief is just stealing random things? It's all a big distraction?"

"Maybe."

"But a distraction for what?" Dread settles over me. Why would the thief be distracting us? Could it really be that we're spending all this time worrying about all these little things going missing, and all the while, the thief is planning a much bigger heist—or something even worse?

I don't like the sound of that.

"Hayley?" calls another voice. "You in there?"

I stand. Cody, Aubrey, and Amelia peek into the woods. Cody's white-blond hair glows in the sunlight, and Aubrey's orange soccer sweatshirt is as bright as a traffic cone.

"Hey," I call out. "I'm coming." I turn back to Siobhan. "Thank you. This is all really...interesting."

Siobhan nods. "I hope I've been helpful."

Then her eyes settle closed. Back to meditating, I guess.

I push out of the woods and meet my friends.

Quickly, I explain to them what Siobhan just suggested, including how she pulled the quarter out from behind my ear.

"A distraction," Aubrey whispers. "You know, that could make sense. Maybe someone is just creating chaos to keep us all occupied. Our eyes aren't on the ball."

"But what does that mean?" I ask. "Is the thief going to steal something huge next? Something right under our noses?" I can't imagine what that might be.

"Or what if it's something even bigger?" Amelia suggests. "Something that will affect all of Silver Screen Studios? Maybe things on other sets have gone missing? Because if it's something bigger this person is planning, they'd want to tie up security too."

My head is spinning. This feels like more than I can handle.

"There's only one thing to do. We need to ask Timothy," Amelia declares, referring to the Silver Screen Studios head of security. Timothy is her close personal friend. With that, Amelia hitches Thena higher on her shoulder and leads the way.

There's nothing for my friends and me to do but follow.

♂ ♀

When we get to the little security booth near the front of the studio, Timothy greets Amelia happily. Then they waste a few minutes discussing their latest interest, the Chinese zodiac. It's based on your birth year. Apparently, they are both Year of the Rabbit, but Timothy is a "Fire Rabbit," meaning he's responsible, while Amelia is a "Metal Rabbit," meaning she's kind, lively, and very honest.

I tap my toe. Is this really important right now?

Amelia turns to me. "What's your Chinese zodiac sign, Hayley? It might be important to this investigation."

"Investigation?" Timothy cocks his head. "What are you kids looking into now?"

"Nothing really," I say carefully, suddenly worried

that Timothy might tell Paul. "But we were just wondering...have robberies been reported on other sets?"

"Or has anything else weird happened?" Cody pipes up. "Anything at all keeping security busy?"

Timothy crosses his arms. "There was a fight on that baking show filming over on Stage Twelve. Someone reported seeing a suspicious "lump" by the back lot and thought it was a dead body. But when we got there, we didn't find anything." He chuckles. "Overdramatic actors! Oh, and then there's Stage Twenty-one."

"That's where the top secret movie is shooting, right?" I whisper.

He looks back and forth shiftily. "You didn't hear it from me."

"Can't you tell us who the actors are on that movie?" Amelia begs. "Pretty please?"

Timothy shakes his head. "Afraid I can't. Could get me fired!" His walkie-talkie bleeps, and he frowns. "Speaking of which, I should probably get going."

"Wait!" Cody says, catching his arm. "Is there anything at all you can tell us about the thief on our set? Any leads? Any idea where Hayley's ring went?"

Timothy's keys are looped around his thumb, and as he shifts his wrist, they jangle noisily. "To tell you the truth, I'm totally stumped about those thefts on the *Sadie* set. I'm afraid that unless we catch the person, they're going to keep happening."

"What?" Aubrey glances down at a gold bracelet on her wrist. It was a gift from her grandmother. I notice Cody touch the beaded necklace he wears. His little brother made it for him.

"But you have no idea who it could be?" I ask.

Timothy shakes his head. "Not yet. To be honest, they're the most puzzling thefts this studio has ever seen."

CHAPTER FOURTEEN

"CODY, HAS ANYONE TOLD YOU THAT YOU'RE THE LUCKIEST KID in the universe?" I call down as I reach the top of the waterslide at Cody's apartment complex. "You literally have a waterslide in your backyard!"

"Don't forget a fro-yo machine, a movie theater, *and* a vintage PacMan arcade machine," Cody says with a smirk.

He's treading water in the splashdown area at the bottom of the slide. I make my way down, careening into the cool, refreshing water with a happy shriek. I come to the surface just in time to see Aubrey topple off the aqua ropes course in the deep end. Aubrey had already mastered the ropes course. This time, she'd been attempting to do it with only her left hand and right leg—*and* with her eyes closed.

After we swim, the three of us settle at a picnic table, big towels wrapped around our shoulders. One of Cody's moms, Jada, brings us a plate of homemade empanadas, which are little pies with meat inside. Cody's little brother, Teddy, splashes in the kiddie area with his new best friend, Jax, who also lives in the complex.

I'm so happy for Cody and his fam. They were so sick of being apart. I'd hate to be away from my family too. But they were also afraid to move to LA. What happened if Cody didn't get another role on a show? What happened if he wanted to quit acting? I can't imagine how many times they went back and forth, trying to figure out what worked best for their family. But in the end, his moms decided to take the plunge and come. It was a daring move, and I can't be more grateful. I'd cry for days if Cody left. Sometimes, as a kid working on a TV show, you don't like your costars at *all*, and it's a lonely life. But I'm surrounded with friends every minute. I'm pretty much the luckiest kid ever.

Well, aside from Cody, who has a waterslide in his backyard.

Thinking about risk-taking and gratitude makes me think of *another* risk that needs to be taken. I turn to Aubrey as she bites into an empanada. "Have you figured out when the auditions are for *Sing Your Heart*?"

Aubrey swallows, dabs at her mouth, and then nods. "They're in a few days and I'm going to go."

"That's amazing!" Cody and I cry at the same time. "Can we go with you?"

"It's okay," Aubrey says. "My mom's bringing me. We sorted out my brother's soccer. She laughed when I even used that as an excuse. She said a musical was a really huge deal, and it was about time someone else hear me sing."

"Uh, *yeah*," Cody says. "We've only been telling you that for the last year!"

Aubrey shrugs like she hasn't heard him. "I figure, the worst thing that happens is I try out and they don't cast me. It's certainly happened before."

"Don't set yourself up for rejection, think positive!" I tell her. "As soon as they hear you sing, they'll absolutely *have* to cast you."

"You *sing*, Aubrey?" comes a voice.

Amelia steps out of the pool's changing room. As usual, Thena is on her shoulder, except now the bearded dragon is wearing the world's tiniest bikini. The bikini has yellow and white stripes, and it perfectly matches the one Amelia is wearing. I can feel Cody rolling his eyes. I'm pretty sure he doesn't quite understand why I let Amelia join our squad, but I keep my promises. Also, I still feel guilty for accusing Amelia. So what if we have to put up with her for a while? Her lizard really *is* adorable.

"Aubrey, you sing?" Amelia repeats as she takes a seat next to us.. "I sing too!"

"Yes, you've mentioned it a few times to us, Amelia."

"I have?" Amelia pushes her sunglasses on her forehead. "But maybe I didn't mention that I cut a demo with this person who works with Taylor Swift last year. Or, well, she *knows* someone who works with Taylor Swift. Ooh, and I did this amazing music video! Except my mom didn't like the outfit I was wearing, so we'll have to reshoot it." Then her eyes go wide. "Ooh, would you want to sing something together sometime, Aubrey? Like even just for TikTok?"

"Uh..." Aubrey starts, looking overwhelmed.

"Or maybe not," Amelia cuts her off. "I prefer to work alone, actually. It's just my Aquarian nature, I think. Like, I can't even imagine having backup dancers when I go on tour. I want it just to be me, on the stage, alone, a single spotlight on my head."

Cody nudges me under the table, and I stifle a giggle. Amelia has barely recorded a song yet, and she's already thinking of backup dancers and a tour?

"*Any*way," Aubrey says, reaching for an empanada, "maybe we should talk about our problem at hand. The thefts."

"Right." I sit up straighter. But I'm not sure what to say. I feel as stumped as Timothy in security does. "I'm so worried more things are going to get stolen. I don't want any of *your* things going missing."

"I know," Cody says, glancing down at the beaded necklace Teddy made him. "And it's an interesting idea that maybe our thief is trying to distract us while they're planning something bigger, but I just can't imagine what that would be—or that we'd have that sort of mastermind on the Silver Screen Studios set, working right under everyone's noses."

"Agreed," Aubrey says. "I really *like* it being a mastermind, though. That sounds so...*action movie*."

"Maybe whoever it is does really just want money," I suggest. "But maybe they got scared after Amelia's mom's earrings went missing—like maybe they thought someone saw them. So they put them back—except in my trailer. Maybe they weren't trying to frame me or Vee, it just sort of happened that my trailer was the first one they saw."

"But why would they steal your ring after that?" Aubrey asks. "And do you think they still have the other piece?" Aubrey asks. "Could we call around to pawn shops or jewelry stores, see if the crown or your ring turned up anywhere?"

Cody motions that he wants to speak. He's got a mouthful of food, but once he swallows, he says, "I overheard Lucinda telling Paul that she has calls into pawn shops and jewelry stores. Nothing has turned up. They're running out of time to film Princess Stella's first scene, and they're going to have to figure out another crown for her."

"Speaking of Princess Stella," I say, "who do we think her secret sister is in Sadie's town? I can't figure it out!"

"I bet it's Gisele," Aubrey says. "The ballet teacher. She seems *so* glamorous."

"Yeah, but Gisele's nearly seventy years old," I remind her. "I'm not sure it makes sense for her to be Stella's secret twin."

"It's totally someone right under our nose, just like we say in the show," Cody says.

"Who, Stella's sister?" I ask, turning to him.

Cody shakes his head. "*No.* The jewel thief. This all keeps happening during the day, when there are people on set. It's someone we know. Maybe even someone we *trust.*"

I can't help but think Cody is right. Problem is, I *hate* that he's right. I hate that someone we trust feels the need to steal. Even worse, I can't come up with who that someone might be.

"How are we going to figure out who this is if we don't have any suspects?" I ask the group. "How can we stop this from happening again?"

Amelia's eyes light up. "Actually, maybe that's just the thing. Maybe we *don't* stop it from happening again."

"We just let something else get stolen?" Aubrey doesn't understand. "I don't like the sound of that."

Amelia shakes her head. "We let something get stolen...because we *know* it's going to be stolen." She grins around at us, and suddenly I know what she's getting at. *This* is the reason we have Amelia around. She might be annoying at times, but she comes up with good ideas.

Amelia leans in closer and says the thing I've already guessed. "We'll plant something for the thief to take... and then we'll watch the thief take it. We'll catch them *red -handed!*"

CHAPTER FIFTEEN

"Cut!" Monique the director calls out the next day.

I let go of the fake windowsill I'd been hanging from. Actually, I'm not hanging at all—the props people brought me a scaffold to stand on to rest my arms, but with the magic of filmmaking and close-ups, it only *looks* like I'm hanging on for dear life. Above me, Aubrey pokes her head out the window and crosses her eyes.

In the scene, Sadie and Kiki sneak into Gigi McIntire's house. Gigi is a very fancy woman in town who owns a clothing boutique, and when Sadie and her pals went back to the courthouse and looked through the records, they discovered that Gigi had been adopted the very same year that Princess Stella was born. Maybe she's the secret sister!

But the only way to prove it is to get a DNA sample and see if Gigi and Stella are a match. Sometimes, you can get DNA samples by swabbing the inside of a person's cheek or taking a lock of their hair, but Gigi is pretty unfriendly and would wonder what Sadie and her pals were up to. So the plan is to sneak in and steal her toothbrush. Before we can both get inside, Gigi returns from an outing. That's why I'm dangling out the window.

When Monique and Paul walk over, they look frazzled. "Not your best performance, ladies," Monique says. "Hayley, Sadie has been in a lot of sticky situations, but you look almost relaxed. You need to be a little more panicked. It's a long drop! You could get hurt!"

"Oh. Sorry." I feel my face redden. It's Monique's job as director to tweak how we act, but I have a feeling she's politely telling me that my head isn't totally in the game.

"And Aubrey, you missed two lines." Monique frowns. "What's with you girls today?"

But I know what's with us. Operation Red-Handed has begun, and I can't think of much else. At this very moment, our thief might be striking again. I want to be there when he or she does.

"Sorry," Aubrey says. "Let's do another take, Monique. We'll nail it, I'm sure."

Monique gives us both a look that says *she* isn't sure, but eventually she and Paul return to the camera. When she calls "Action!" again, I focus on Sadie and the task at hand. I'm not standing on a scaffold, I'm really dangling from a window. I channel fear. I strain my arms to hold on. I'm so in the moment, my fingers cramp and my heart speeds up.

"Hurry," I yell to Aubrey. "Find the bathroom! Grab the toothbrush!"

"Oops, that's a closet," Aubrey says, nailing a line

she'd missed before. She disappears for a moment and then returns looking triumphant, holding a red toothbrush high. "Got it!"

Aubrey runs over and hurtles out the window, nearly knocking me over. Her comic timing is perfect, and I can tell Monique likes it too because she's grinning behind the camera.

"And scene!" Paul shouts from around the wall. The bell rings. That means the cameras are no longer rolling and people around the soundstage are free to make noise. Monique gives us a thumbs-up, and I breathe a sigh of relief.

"Good job, ladies," Monique says. *"That's* what I want to see."

The moment the sound techs unwind the microphones from Aubrey and me, we're out of Stage Five in a flash. My heart pounds as I approach my trailer door. *What if the thief is in there right now? What if we catch him in the act?*

I push the door open. But the trailer is empty.

Aubrey's shoulders slump. "Boo." Even more surprising, *nothing* is gone.

This morning, each of us brought a bunch of jewelry from home. I gathered up a few silver pieces of my mom's along with a locket she gave me for Christmas last year. Cody added his beaded necklace, and Aubrey reluctantly forked over her gold bracelet. Amelia added the Sadie necklace. As the icing on the cake, we even threw in this shiny geode I found on the set. We're looking for maximum sparkle factor—something that will really lure a thief. There isn't much risk involved, since the moment the stuff is taken, we'll know exactly who took it.

Earlier, we arranged the stuff in a pile on my side table. I even left my trailer door a teensy bit open so that anyone passing by would see the jewelry. I also made sure to talk very loudly about how I was doing a shoot for a jewelry brand after my scenes today and had a lot of good pieces in my trailer. Before we all went to hair and makeup and to film our scenes, we rigged a tiny camera at the door. It's connected to an app on our phones, and an alarm will go off if the camera detects any movement.

"How is this possible?" I stare at the untouched pile of jewels. "Everyone knows the jewels are here." I glance over at Salmon, who's lying on the couch, casually licking his paws. "Did *you* see anyone?"

Salmon just blinks.

Cody and Amelia burst into the trailer. "Did anything happen?" Cody cries excitedly.

"No," I mutter. "Nothing's missing."

I slump onto the couch and rewind the security app. Timothy helped install it. We'd sort of had to fudge why we needed such a thing, as we didn't want him to tell Paul we were secretly investigating this case, so I'd said that I was making a short film about Salmon and wanted footage of him doing cat stuff when no one was looking.

The app shows no movement. Even Salmon barely stirs. It's the most boring video ever.

"Maybe we're being too obvious?" Amelia says. "Like, maybe the thief doesn't want to come into your trailer again, Hayley, because after the earrings showed up here *and* your ring went missing, they figure you might be watching."

"We move the jewels to my trailer instead?" a voice calls behind us. "No one will think *I'm* in on this."

I'm thrilled to see Vee in the doorway. She's back! I lunge forward and give her a huge hug. The others do too. Vee starts to giggle.

"Whoa, whoa!" she cries. "Let me breathe!" Then she adds, "I'm serious about putting those jewels in my trailer. You're trying to catch the thief, right?"

"Well, yeah," Amelia says sheepishly. "But please don't tell Paul."

Vee pretends to zip up her lips and lock them with a key. "I think it's a great idea. I want to catch this thief too."

It isn't hard to move the pile of jewels or the camera, and in ten minutes, we've installed everything in Vee's makeup trailer. Then, Vee also introduces us to her new assistant—Elizabeth, the former PA. "Elizabeth is going to help me with makeup from now on," Vee says. "I'm going to teach her everything I know."

"That's amazing!" I cry.

"Right? I was dying without Vee here." Elizabeth beams. "I've also agreed to do the makeup of some of the more difficult actors." She hides a laugh. "Like Wendy Bongiovanni."

We all groan, remembering how Wendy wants to do her makeup herself.

"And don't worry, Elizabeth will keep our secret," Vee adds, sneaking a peek in the direction of one of the cameras. "She's like a vault."

"Keep a secret about what?"

Oops. Paul has paused on the pavement just outside the trailer, and he's looking at us suspiciously. My mouth goes dry.

"Uh, about..." I start, but I can't think of anything.

"About Thena!" Amelia blurts. "It's a secret about Thena!" She moves closer to Paul and whispers, *"She's having a baby."*

Paul gets a weird look. His gaze shifts to the lizard. I wonder if he's questioning *how* lizards have babies. Do they lay eggs? Do they have a litter of lizards, like dogs or cats? I don't have a clue.

Eventually, he just walks away. The six of us, Vee and Elizabeth included, look at each other and burst out laughing.

"You definitely weirded him out, Amelia," Vee says.

Lunch break is ending, and we all need to get back on set. I click the app to test the cameras out one more time. Everything is working. Excitement churns in my belly once more. Maybe Amelia is right—planting the jewels in my trailer *was* too obvious. Vee's trailer will be empty for the rest of the day. Aubrey, Cody and I also made sure people could overhear us talking about putting the jewels there. It's the perfect opportunity for someone to sneak in and steal the loot. I never thought I'd say this, but I hope the jewel thief strikes again.

♂ ♀

After the rest of our scenes that afternoon, we race back to Vee's makeup trailer, pushing the door open. It's easy to do, since Vee didn't lock it. The cat door she installed for Salmon bangs.

To our astonishment, the pile of jewels is *still there*. All of us are agape. There's practically a neon sign over the stuff, begging the thief to take it!

I whirl around and look at Aubrey, Cody, Amelia, and Vee, saying jokingly, "Is one of *you* the thief? It seems like they're tracking our every move."

Vee checks her watch. "I need to get home. Ava has a pre-op appointment for her surgery in an hour." She glances at the pile of jewels and shrugs. "I'm so annoyed we didn't catch him."

We wish Vee good luck with Ava's appointment, and then all of us head home too. My mom is waiting in the parking lot. I slump into the back of her car, plop Salmon's cat carrier in the footwell, and rest my head against the seat. My mom turns around and peers at me curiously.

"You okay, Hayley? You look like you had a terrible day."

I sigh. By most accounts, I had a great day.

But I still haven't solved the mystery.

CHAPTER SIXTEEN

THE MOMENT I GET OUT OF MY PARENTS' CAR AT THE STUDIO LOT
the following morning, Vee barrels toward me, her eyes wide.

"Hayley! The jewels are *gone*!"

"What?" I nearly walk off without shutting the car
door. My parents give me a curious look, probably wondering what Vee is talking about. I wave back at them, and
finally my dad drives off.

I fall in step with Vee as she walks back to her trailer.
"All of them. *Gone.* It must have happened in the middle of
the night."

"That's great!" I *knew* the thief would strike eventually.

I pull my phone from my bag, surprised I hadn't gotten an alert from the app that the cameras had picked up movement. I couldn't wait to see who the thief was.

During the thirty seconds it takes the app to load, Aubrey, Cody, and Amelia walk beside us. Vee tells them the news. Finally, the app's camera feed appears. I stare at the view of Vee's trailer door. I rewind the footage, waiting until I see a blip of movement. But that's the weird thing. I rewind the video all the way back to yesterday, when Vee says she left for the day. The door doesn't move all night. No one even walked past the camera.

Huh?

By this time, we've reached Vee's trailer. I step inside and look around. Just like Vee said, the pile of jewels is gone. I look around her cluttered workspace, checking out the mirrors, the shelves, and the seats. Unlike my trailer, Vee's doesn't have a window.

"How did someone get in here without it showing up on the camera?" I whisper.

"Maybe there *is* a ghost," Aubrey says, but she doesn't look very amused anymore.

I sniff the air. It smells familiar—nutty, maybe. But I can't figure why.

"Maybe we should have positioned the camera on the jewels, not on the door," Vee says.

She seems to realize something else, and she turns to Aubrey and Cody, looking like she might cry. "All your stuff is gone. Your bracelet."

"My necklace too," Amelia says quietly.

And my mom's jewelry, I think, feeling sick. And the locket she gave me for Christmas.

"I thought we'd know who took it and get it back immediately," Vee says. "I let you down by bringing everything into my trailer." She reaches for her own phone. "We need to report that it's missing."

"Wait," Aubrey touches her wrist. "You're the only one on the security cams—again. I don't want them to suspect *you,* Vee."

"That's true," Cody agrees. "We don't want you to get in trouble. Not with Ava's surgery coming up."

Vee's eyes water. "I'm just so sorry."

I turn and stare at the door, still puzzled. How could this have happened? And our stuff—is it all *gone*?

Salmon's cat carrier starts to shake, which is my cat's sign that he's getting restless. "Behave," I scold as let him out. Salmon jumps out of the carrier and darts over to the little cat door Vee installed. I watch as he sniffs it curiously. Then he turns around and stares at me.

"Don't even think about leaving," I tell him. The last thing I need is having a set-wide search for my cat. I scoop him up in my arms and then look at the cat door again. Could the thief have squeezed through that? The camera is facing the top of the door, not the bottom. But it's so small. Who on the set would be small enough?

A knock on the door surprises us. When the door flies open, it's Paul, and he has Lucinda in tow. They look frantic. There are big splotches on Lucinda's cheeks.

"There's been another theft," Lucinda blurts.

"What?" I cry. "*Two* thefts in one morning?"

"Hold on, hold on," Paul says. "Let's not get ahead of ourselves. Maybe there's an explanation. Has anyone seen a geode? Rock on the outside, but beautiful crystal on the inside? It was near Video Village?"

A geode? *Uh -oh.*

I must make a tiny whimper, because Paul turns to me. "What is it, Hayley? Have you seen it? We need it for the shoot later. It's very important. And valuable."

"I..." My heart starts to pound. The back of my neck starts to sweat. I can't lie. "I took it! I was trying to lure the thief, and we laid all the stuff out and tried to film them, but something screwed up! But now it's...it's *gone*!"

Paul just stares. Then, he slowly shakes his head. "Didn't I tell you not to get in the middle of this, Hayley?"

"Yes," I say in a near whisper. "But—"

"Didn't I tell you to leave it to the experts?" he adds.

"Yes," I squeak again. "*But—*"

"It's our fault too," Aubrey pipes up. "We were all in on this, not just Hayley."

"Yeah," Cody adds. "Well. All except Vee."

Paul runs his hands through his hair. "And now the geode is gone. Do you know how much that geode was worth?"

"Uh..." My voice trembles.

Paul groans. "This is great. Just great."

I feel a lump in my throat. I've never seen Paul so upset. "I'm sorry, Paul," I whisper. "I really was just trying to help."

"You were supposed to *listen*." He looks at me sadly. "You need to stop your investigation right now, Hayley. Okay? Or we'll have to fire you."

I gasp. "*Fire* me?"

Amelia straightens. "You can't fire her! She's the star of your show! And if you fire her, I'll quit too!"

Paul blinks. Then he rubs his eyes, perhaps realizing that what he said makes no sense. "Sorry. We won't fire you. Still, you'll be in trouble. *All* of you. Got it?"

And then, without waiting for our answer, he spins around, marches out of the trailer, and slams the door hard.

"Got it," I say quietly and feel the tears roll down my cheeks.

CHAPTER SEVENTEEN

"ANOTHER COOKIE?" AUBREY ASKS, HOLDING OUT THE TIN.

"I'm too sad to eat," I mumble, staring at her delicious homemade cookies. Aubrey likes to stress bake sometimes. Right now, I wish I could stress eat too. But I'm so worked up by what just happened. Paul's never yelled at me like that. And the idea of me getting fired—it's unthinkable! I love working on *Sadie Solves It*. I don't want to leave my friends.

The idea that all of our stuff is missing is also weighing on me. "How do we keep running into dead ends?" I ask my friends. "Who took our things?"

Cody shakes his head. "Hayley, I think you have to let it go."

"It's not so easy," I say. "We're *all* missing stuff that means a lot to us. I can't help but think that's kind of my fault...and that I should be the one to make this right."

"We all decided to put our stuff in that pile," Aubrey reminds me. "You didn't force us to do it."

I know she's right, but it still doesn't make me feel any better. We laid a foolproof trap, and still the thief tricked us. How did someone steal those jewels without getting through Vee's front door? *Did* they use the cat door? Is it possible?

"Maybe we should distract ourselves by looking at today's scenes?" Amelia suggests, holding up the scripts that one of the PAs has delivered while we were talking to Paul. "I think Sadie solves who Princess Stella's long-lost sister is."

"Really?" I reach for one of the scripts. I've been dying to know who that might be.

Soon enough, all of us are skimming the lines to get to the good part. Cody, who is a speed-reader, gets there first. He gasps. "*What*? No way."

Then I read the lines too. The DNA results for Gigi's toothbrush came in, and she wasn't the secret sister. Neither was Marley Morales, who stars in all the community theater plays, and Tasha Smith, who runs a dog-walking business—they're the only other babies who were adopted that same year. Actually, there is a record of a fourth baby girl who'd been adopted that year, but no one in town recognizes her name.

However, when Sadie spoke with Madame Curio, the psychic had a *vision*. Maybe this fourth adopted baby *changed* her name. So Sadie goes back through the records, and it all comes together. Turns out, Mrs. Stein, the school principal, changed her name when she was eighteen. *And* she's the princess's age. Sadie and the others secretly snip a lock of her hair when she's sitting in a school board meeting. They rush it to their scientist friend at the lab, and when the results come in, they're positive!

"Princess Stella's long-lost sister really *was* under our noses the whole time," Aubrey says when she finishes reading. "I wonder what Wendy thinks about this?"

I think about the grumpy actress and how excited she got when she met Amelia's bearded dragon. Then I close the script pages, something catching in my mind. "Princess Stella's sister was under our noses. The thief has got to be too. It's just someone we're not thinking of."

"Hayley," Cody says in a singsong voice. "Didn't you hear me? We need to let it go."

"Or maybe some*thing* we're not thinking of," I add, not listening.

Aubrey raises an eyebrow. "What do you mean?"

"Let's think of the clues one more time. Someone's climbing through windows. Someone's freaking out Salmon. Someone's taking jewelry but then putting it back."

"Meaning someone might not need money," Amelia suggests.

"I can't stop thinking about Salmon sniffing that cat door in Vee's trailer either," I say. "Salmon's not like a dog. He doesn't sniff at something unless it's really interesting."

"So...it's someone that could fit through a cat door? And someone who has a smell?" Cody looks unsure. "Is it a child? Do they wear a lot of perfume? Or who walks around with cookies in their pockets?"

"Salmon isn't that motivated by food," I say. "To be honest, he's mostly into the way other animals smell. Dogs...cats...birds..."

"But there aren't animals at Silver Screen Studios," Amelia says. "This isn't a zoo."

That's when I get it. It must hit Aubrey and Cody at the same time, because all of us sit up straighter.

There *are* animals at Silver Screen Studios. *Animals Extraordinaire.*

At that very moment, Salmon lets out a low growl. His

tail is puffed up again, and he's staring at the back window. When I turn, I let out a shriek. All I can see is a pair of glowing eyes on the other side!

"Guys," I whisper, my heart picking up speed. "W-what is that out there?"

Salmon takes a few careful steps toward the blinking eyes, still making that weird growling sound. At the same time, Amelia's lizard makes a strange noise too. A sort of hissing noise. When I turn to her, I see that the bottom of her neck is puffed up, and her mouth is wide open.

"Amelia?" I say cautiously. "Thena isn't poisonous, is she?"

But Amelia doesn't answer. Her gaze is on the window. That's when I turn and see it too. The figure, whatever it might be, is *holding something*. Something shiny. Something *silver*.

It's my Sadie ring!

"That's it!" I cry, nudging my friends and pointing to the window. "That's the thief!"

At that moment, Salmon springs for the window and disappears through a tiny crack.

"Salmon!" Aubrey cries, rushing for the window.

But Salmon is gone.

CHAPTER EIGHTEEN

"CATCH HIM!" I SCREAM AS I FLY OUT OF MY TRAILER. WHAT
is Salmon *thinking*? Silver Screen Studios isn't an eight-
lane highway, but there are always golf carts whizzing past.
If he runs off beyond the soundstage, he could get hurt!

Aubrey sprints ahead, chasing Salmon down the corridor between Stage Five and Stage Six. An assistant on a
bicycle whizzes past in the other direction, and the two of
them almost collide.

"Hey!" the assistant cries.

After sidestepping the guy, we've lost sight of Salmon

again. Then I notice his tail vanishing around yet another corner. He's heading toward the spooky woods.

"C'mon!" I yell to my friends. "Let's go!"

We hurry around the bend. My lungs burn from running hard. Salmon's tail bobs. And as I look ahead of *him*, I spy whatever Salmon is chasing. Something dark whips into the trees. There's a *whoosh* as Salmon dives into the bushes too.

I pause, breathing hard, listening to where Salmon could have gone. The rustling stops. I peer into the bush, terrified that my cat hurt himself.

"Salmon?" I call. "Are you okay?"

"Did you see that thing he's chasing?" Amelia comes up behind me. "It looked like a rat! It had a long tail!"

"We're giving ourselves heart attacks chasing after a rat?" Cody leans over his knees to catch his breath. "I thought it was the thief!"

"I think it *is* the thief," I insist. "I swear it was holding my ring."

Cody squints at me. "A rat stole our stuff?"

But before I can answer, there's a *rrrowww*, followed by a crash. Salmon leaps through the air. The swiftly moving jewel thief zooms away too. In seconds, they're on the other side of the woods.

"Come on!" I yell to my friends, sprinting down the rocky path.

I can barely keep up with Salmon as he races down "Main Street" in the back lot, which is made up to look like the quaint little town Sadie lives in. A few people from the art department are fixing one of the storefronts, and they gawk at us as we run past. Halfway down the block, I've lost Salmon again.

I turn back to the art department people. "Did you see a cat run by just now?"

One of the guys points down an alley. "Think he went in there."

I head in that direction, passing the pizza shop, Gigi McIntire's boutique, and a few of the actors and staff.

Among them is...*Paul*. Oh no. *Oh no.* And he sees me. Now he's coming over.

"Hayley?" Paul blinks hard. He doesn't look happy. "What's going on?"

My mouth feels dry. I don't know how to answer. If Paul finds out I'm after the thief again, what if I get in trouble? What if I get *fired*?

Amelia comes to my rescue. "Her cat got out! We have to save him!"

Paul widens his eyes and steps aside. I sprint to the

end of the block and turn into the alley. We use this alley-way for scenes sometimes, and it's decorated to look really creepy. There are spiderwebs, brick walls covered in graf-fiti, trash cans overflowing with fake garbage, and even a few fake rats. But I hear squeaks and rustles too. I look right and left, terrified a *real* rodent is about to run across my foot.

"Salmon?" I call out. "Here, boy! Come out? Please?"

An annoyed *meow* rings out. I breathe a sigh of relief, happy that at least Salmon is here.

"Salmon?" I take a step into the alley. "Where are you, fella?"

"Is that him?" Paul calls. He's followed us in here. "Want me to help you grab him?"

Crash. Several garbage cans fall over. I shriek and jump back, grabbing Aubrey's arm. It's way too dark. I have a feeling that whatever Salmon was chasing is in this alley too. But I don't actually know what the thing *is*. It could be anything. Maybe something unthinkable. Like some kind of...*monster.*

Meow, Salmon says again. His voice echoes.

"Come on, Salmon," I beg. "L-let's get out of here. Want a treat?"

Something flies past my body. I let out another scream and cover my face, feeling a pair of feathery wings brush against my cheek.

A bird. That's all it is. It must have been hiding back here.

"I see Salmon!" Amelia cries. "He's there!"

She turns on the flashlight app on her cell phone and shines it against the bricks. I can just make out my cat's dark, slinky shape and his bright, glowing eyes. Salmon has something cornered. It looks like an animal is trapped at the end of the alley, frozen in fear.

I blink, realizing I *know* this animal. I take in its big eyes and small head. I take in its long fingers and toes and sparkly pink tutu.

"Jojo?" I blurt. "The monkey?"

Jojo glares at us. And then, I notice something else. Something that makes me gasp. Just behind Jojo, pushed against the wall, is a large pile of objects. As the beam of Amelia's flashlight shines across it, the silver glitters. The jewels sparkle. The gold shines.

It's all our stuff. We found the thief!

CHAPTER NINETEEN

"Jojo," Cody says in a calm voice, not making any sudden moves. "It's okay. We're not going to hurt you."

Jojo's gaze shifts to Salmon, who still has him cornered. It's funny to think that my cat is bossing around a much larger animal, but then again, Salmon's claws *are* pretty sharp. And don't get me started on his teeth.

"I can't believe it," Paul mutters. "A *monkey* did all of this? It's all there. The crown, the geode, all the jewels... It's incredible!"

"Yeah, but how are we going to *get* to the stuff?" Amelia asks, sounding worried.

She's right. Jojo is guarding his treasure and shows no signs of moving. We're stuck.

Then I hear footsteps. "Jojo!" a voice cries. Behind us is Andrew the animal trainer, the same guy we saw on the *Animals Extraordinaire* set—*and* the guy who let that kangaroo drive his golf cart.

"Can you help us?" Amelia asks. "He's back there, and he won't come out."

Andrew rushes past us, breathing hard. "*There* you are, Jojo! What are you doing over here? How did you get out of your cage?"

"I think he's been getting out of his cage a lot," I tell him. "Sneaking through windows and cat doors...and he gathered quite a few interesting objects from the *Sadie* set. That crown is important for our current episode."

Andrew looks embarrassed. "Jojo is smart—and he hates to be in that cage. I feel bad for him—and all the animals—so I keep them out of their cages as much as possible."

"Yeah, you let them ride around on golf carts," Aubrey jokes.

"True," Andrew says. "But usually they're very obedient. Jojo is mischievous. We've been noticing he's been stealing shiny stuff on the set—random coins, someone's car keys—but we've been able to catch him before he hides any of it. He must have gotten tired of getting caught, though. So he moved onto your set instead." He clucks his tongue at Jojo. "And look at you, hiding all of this stuff in this alley! You must have really worried the *Sadie* team!"

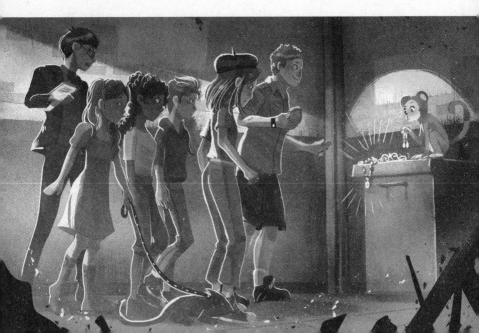

"It was pretty confusing," Aubrey admits. "We were starting to think we had a ghost again!"

Andrew shakes his head and looks at Paul. "I'm so sorry to cause all this trouble."

"No worries," Paul says. "I'm just happy we figured it out. Well. The *kids* figured it out. I had nothing to do with it." He looks at me. "Hayley, I owe you a huge apology. I should have never blown up at you like I did this morning, even if you wouldn't have solved this. But this is huge. The crown is back. The geode. I can't thank you enough."

I shrug. "Everyone helped. Cody. Aubrey. Amelia. Vee. Salmon."

"Even Thena!" Amelia adds, gesturing to the lizard on her shoulder.

"Your pets are honorary members of the Silver Screen Sleuthios for sure," Aubrey says.

Paul frowns. "The Silver Screen *Sleuthios*?"

I sigh. "I guess that's our name now."

"I love it!" Amelia cries.

I can't believe it, but I sort of do too.

Paul turns to Andrew. "But we're going to need some of those items for our shoot pretty soon. Think Jojo's going to give them up?"

"Oh sure." Andrew reaches into his pocket and pulls something out. "Jojo! Snack!"

Jojo perks up. I peer at the object in the trainer's hand. My instincts tell me it's probably a banana—the perfect monkey treat, right? But to my surprise, it's what looks like a peanut butter and jelly sandwich.

Peanut butter. That explains the nutty smell in my trailer!

Andrew waves the sandwich. "Jojo can't get enough of these. They're my secret weapon."

Jojo takes a cautious step away from his pile of loot. Salmon hisses, but I warn him to behave. The monkey tiptoes past. Andrew extends his arm, and just as Jojo grabs the sandwich, the trainer grabs *him*.

"Gotcha," Andrew says. "No more stealing for you, my friend."

Everyone cheers. We rush forward and grab our stolen items. Paul picks up the crown and the geode. Aubrey, Amelia, and Cody get their bracelets and necklaces. I scoop up my mom's silver jewelry and the locket she gave me for Christmas. But when I look around, I don't see my Sadie ring. My heart starts to pound. Did Jojo hide it somewhere else?

"Oops," Andrew says. He pries something from the monkey's fingers. "C'mon, Jojo. Give it up."

Finally, he wrenches the object free. The silver glimmers. My ring! I let out a squeal and leap for it, sliding it back on my finger. I'm never taking this thing off again!

"Sorry about that," Andrew says. "Guess Jojo thought your ring was especially important."

"It *is* important," I tell the monkey gently. "I feel the same way."

CHAPTER TWENTY

"WHO WANTS TO CUT THE CAKE?" MONIQUE, OUR DIRECTOR, calls out. She's holding a big silver knife and standing in front of a delicious-looking three-tier vanilla cake that reads *Sadie Solves It* in wiggly letters on the top.

"Me!" Amelia says, bustling to the front. "I have a very steady hand. All Aquarians do."

I groan under my breath. *Typical Amelia.* But then I catch myself. I'm supposed to be cutting Amelia some slack. After all, Amelia was the first person who stood up for me when Paul got mad. She really *is* a good friend, even if she's way too into astrology.

The whole cast and crew of *Sadie Solves It* has gathered in Stage Five for a party. It's sort of a wrap party—we've finished shooting the second episode—and it's also a celebration that all of our jewelry and props have been recovered. It's also a celebration for Vee, who not only is our makeup artist again—all her charges were dropped—but because her daughter, Ava, came through her cochlear implant procedure with flying colors. In fact, Ava is here today, blinking in wonderment at everything she can now clearly hear. Vee holds her hand tightly, her eyes rimmed with proud, relieved tears.

And finally, it's a party celebrating the *Fangirl* cover article—copies are stacked on tables so everyone can read the story. I glance at the cover. It's funny to see the picture of us from that day. Just minutes after Bruce snapped those photos, Jojo the monkey stole the crown. I've already quickly skimmed through the story to see if Imogen the nosy reporter wrote anything about ghosts or things mysteriously going missing. She hadn't. That made me relieved, but also kind of disappointed. Deep down, I'm proud of the mysteries we've solved, even if they've gotten us in big trouble.

Amelia cuts the cake, making nice, even pieces for everyone. Once we all get a slice, I retreat to the couch and dig in. Aubrey sits next to me, and Amelia and Cody join us too. Even Salmon is at this party, though I have him on a special cat leash so he can't run off. Amelia has Thena on a leash too, and of all things, the cat and lizard are sitting right next to each other, comfortable in one another's company.

"Do you think they're friends?" I ask.

"Maybe?" Amelia swallows a mouthful of cake. "I didn't think reptiles and cats got along, but who knows?"

"They'll have to, considering they're official members of the Silver Screen Sleuthios." Paul walks over, balancing a piece of cake in his hand. "I've already told my writers' room to look out. Soon enough, you guys will be writing the episodes yourselves since you're so good at solving cases."

"No way are we as skilled as the writers," I say. "I'd never have been able to come up with the plot twist that Mrs. Stein the principal is Princess Stella's long-lost twin sister."

"*And* they're new BFFs in real life," Aubrey murmurs, glancing at Wendy Bongiovanni and Brooklyn Bates. They're standing near the doors, laughing their heads off about some private joke. I'm glad Wendy has a new friend, though. She looks so much happier now.

Paul turns to me. "Hayley, would you want to sit in the writers' room for an episode or two? Maybe see how

you like it? I really do think you might have a talent at coming up with mystery ideas."

I think about this for a moment. While it would be fun to come up with *Sadie* plots with the writers, I think I already have my hands full playing the lead. "I want to focus on being Sadie," I tell him. "Especially now that hopefully there aren't any more crimes to solve."

"Maybe not on the *Sadie* set," Aubrey says with a wink, "but people all over Silver Screen Studios heard about us figuring out the ghost thing and that a monkey was a thief. What if there's a mystery on another set? The Silver Screen Sleuthios have to come to the rescue!"

We laugh about that for a minute. I wonder if people all over Silver Screen Studios really have heard about our crime-solving skills. Maybe even the super-famous actors on the top secret movie! I wouldn't mind solving a crime for *them*.

"Speaking of the monkey thief," Cody says, changing the subject, "did you guys hear that Jojo retired?"

"Andrew the trainer told me earlier today," I say. Though Jojo was a great asset to *Animals Extraordinaire*, Andrew had a sense that he just wasn't happy with being in a cage for so much of the time. But apparently, Andrew adopted him, and he's living full-time in Andrew's apartment.

"Do you think Jojo misses being in the spotlight?" I ask. "He really was quite a ham."

"Andrew says they're open to him doing guest appearances," Cody says. "So he'd only come onto set for a day or two. But I wonder who's going to be the star of that show now. Jojo was really talented."

"I'm thinking of having Thena audition," Amelia says. "Though I'm not really sure what her talent might be." Her eyes light up as she looks at me. "Maybe Salmon and Thena should audition together!"

Then, Aubrey clears her throat. "Um, *speaking* of auditions..."

I sit up straighter. "Oh my gosh." In the excitement,

I'd completely forgotten about Aubrey's audition for *Sing Your Heart*. It was yesterday. Or, I *hope* it was yesterday.

"Did you go?" I ask. "What was it like? How did you do? Please say you went. Please say you didn't chicken out." Sometimes, when I get nervous, I blurt out a whole bunch of questions at once without letting the person answer.

"I went," Aubrey says sadly. Her gaze falls to her lap.

My heart sinks. It must not have gone well. "But at least you tried!" I cry. "That's the most important part! And so what if they don't want you? There will be other chances!"

Aubrey looks up, a big, sly grin on her face. "Gotcha!" Her smile is so wide, it stretches practically to her ears. "I got a part, Hayley! I'm going to be in the movie!"

"*What?*" Cody and I scream, jumping up and grabbing her hands. "No way! That is amazing!" Even Amelia, who's often jealous about everything, leaps up with us.

"It's wild, right?" Aubrey giggles. "I just hope I can

make it all work with this show too. It's going to be a busy schedule!"

"You'll make it work," I promise her. "We'll help you."

"I know you will," Aubrey says, and we all move in for a big hug one more time. My heart is bursting with happiness.

As I pull back, my gaze rests on the Sadie ring on my finger. I'm so happy to have it back. Everything truly feels right with the world, actually—everyone is safe, and the mysteries are solved. I'm so relaxed that I almost don't notice the faint scream I hear in the distance. But then I stand up straighter and cock my head. My ears perk up. I brace myself for another scream to come. Has something happened? Something *mysterious?*

I wait for another scream to come, but none does. Must have just been my imagination. I chuckle softly, suddenly realizing something. I really *am* like Sadie.

I'm always ready to solve a mystery. No matter what.

ABOUT THE AUTHOR

 Hayley LeBlanc is a thirteen-year-old actress, artist, and social media star with more than 5.3 million followers across Instagram and YouTube. Hayley performed in the lead role of Harmony in the two hit Brat TV series *Chicken Girls* and *Mani*. Hayley lives in Los Angeles, where in her spare time she likes to hang out with friends, listen to music, read books, and watch horror and mystery films and TV shows.